The Game Called Life

By

Kay Gilley

1stBooks – rev. 05/11/01

**To Dick and Freida
Angels Unaware**

iv

Table of Contents

Chapter One

A World Upside-Down

"What was *that*?" asked Lizzie, her head spinning as she picked herself up off the ground and straightened her clothes like Dorothy unexpectedly arriving in Oz.

"That, my friend, is a wake-up call," said a voice. Lizzie spun on her heels but she couldn't see anyone.

"Who's talking to me?" she asked indignantly.

"Oh, it was me," said the same voice again, but once again she couldn't see anyone...or even figure out what direction it was coming from.

"Maybe I'm crazy," Lizzie thought to herself. "I was sure I heard a voice but there was no one around.

"You did hear a voice, Lizzie."

"First, I'm hearing voices, and then they appear to be reading my mind. Am I losing it completely?" Lizzie asked aloud.

"You're not crazy, Lizzie...and I can read your mind. I'm Helen. I'm a special helper who's been assigned specifically to answer your prayers."

Once again Lizzie looked about, but still no one in sight. "Oh, you won't be able to see me. You must simply have faith that I am here to help you."

Helen continued, "You remember last week when you sat in your car at the stoplight and said, 'I am so tired. If there is a God, help me. There's got to be more to life than this."

"I remember," said Lizzie, still uncomfortable with what felt like talking to herself.

"Well, I'm here to answer your prayers."

"This voice out of nowhere is the answer to my prayers?" she queried. "You could have been a bit more gentle about it. Rolling down that hill on the pavement really hurt. Look, my hand is bleeding, and my running clothes are torn."

"Lizzie, God has been trying to get your attention for six years now, but you've been racing so hard and fast that we gave up on the gentle approach. God's just been waiting for an invitation for more direct action. I would have been here sooner, but I was just finishing another assignment."

"Six years? direct action? finishing another assignment? I don't understand any of this!" Lizzie exclaimed.

"Let me explain. I am assigned to aid mortals who have forgotten what life is all about when they are finally ready to get a life. They usually utter some kind of prayer which they didn't take seriously, like the one last week in your car. They forget that God is always with them and that every single thought is heard as a prayer. That really gets a lot of people in trouble. They worry that something will happen, and then, sure enough it does. Their worries are taken by God as prayers. God is just answering their prayers."

"You mean when I worried about that schmuck that I was married to leaving me for another woman that became a prayer?" Lizzie asked.

"That's exactly right. When he left you with his secretary six years ago, that was your first wake-up call."

"So when you said God had been trying to get my attention for six years, that's what you meant?"

"Well that was the first time, but you kept racing. A bit like that fellow I just finished helping. Bill was 53 years old and working 60 hours a week so that he could send his kids to a prestigious university, but what they really needed was time with him. He kept saying 'I'm just doing what is the best for my kids.' In order to answer his prayer to have what was best for them, his heart finally had an attack so he could spend some time with them," Helen continued.

"You kept saying that after retirement you'd do God's work. Not long after you'd been saying that is when your father was critically ill and died just as he was about to retire. It was an opportunity to discover that life can't be put off till retirement, but Lizzie, you didn't get it."

"And the next year when both my grandmothers, my uncle, and even my dog died, I suppose that was to teach me that none of us lives forever," Lizzie queried.

"That's right. You are catching on now. This may go faster than I thought," Helen said excitedly.

Kay Gilley

"So exactly what was it that you were trying to teach me when you rolled me down that steep hill this morning?" Lizzie wondered.

"Well, last week you noted that there had to be more to life than you'd been living, and you asked God to help you see it."

Lizzie recalled her frustration and disillusionment last week. It seemed like she spent all her time racing from one meaningless event to another. Although she'd experienced material success, she felt empty, like Lizzie had been forgotten somewhere along the line. She now remembered leaning over her steering wheel in tears as she asked for help.

"You've had life upside down. We hoped that tumble would help you turn the world right side up again," Helen continued cheerfully.

"Life upside down? What does *that* mean? I'm just doing what everybody else does. Get a job, a nice place to live, food to eat, reliable transportation, a get-away once or twice a year, and plan responsibly for retirement. You're telling me that's upside-down? That's what all the life-planning seminars tell us to do. I've just been following the rules," Lizzie said. Even though she had known something wasn't right for a long while, she was still a bit exasperated that she might have just wasted 40 years on the wrong thing.

"Oh, those life-planning seminars again. I really don't know what we are going to do about them. They miss the whole point!"

"Miss the whole point?" Lizzie inquired. "If that's not the point, what is?"

"The game!" Helen said, "The game! They forget that The Game Called Life is a *game.*"

"A game?" Lizzie asked, adding, "This is just too weird. I'm walking through my neighborhood at dawn in torn clothes, my hand bleeding, aching in every joint from tumbling on pavement down a steep hill, and talking to someone I can't see who is supposed to help me by telling me that life is really a game."

"It *is* a game. I am here to help you discover what life is about before you die, which was going to happen all too soon at the rate you were going."

"What does *that* mean?"

"It means that people who come to believe so hopelessly in the material world that they forget why they came into the world may get called home early. People get called home early for a variety of reasons, but those who totally lose touch with the point of The Game Called Life get called home early to give them a chance to start over," Helen explained patiently.

Although she'd been walking most of the time they'd been talking, Lizzie was still several blocks from home. She'd been over a mile into her predawn run when she "accidentally" fell. The light rain had stopped now, as it often did just before daybreak, but she was achy, tired, wet, and confused by this whole conversation. Making her way to the curb, she sat down and buried her head in her hands. Tears began streaming down her cheeks, "Hopeless?" she probed.

"You are not as bad as some," Helen responded, "but you have already slept through six years of wake-up calls!"

"I really don't understand all this," Lizzie said, realizing that a neighbor had just spotted her on the curb and stopped.

"You OK, Lizzie? Need a lift?"

"Uh...yeah, I'm OK. I took a bit of a fall down the Fox Hollow hill. I was just walking out some of the stiffness and took a break. I'm ready to walk some more now," Lizzie said, coming to her feet.

"You look like you've been crying. Sure you're OK? I'll take you home if you'd like."

"Yeah. Thanks for the offer, but I'd really like to walk."

As soon as the car was out of ear-shot, Lizzie said, "Helen, my neighbors are going to think I'm crazy."

"Tsk! Tsk! It could be worse."

"And how could that be?" Lizzie wondered.

"You could still be chasing through that fictional world you've created, having totally forgotten it was a game! That's what is really crazy."

"There you go with that game thing again. Have I *really* been nearly hopeless?" Lizzie was on the edge.

"Nearly, my dear, nearly. But not hopeless. You look like you could use a rest. That bench over there looks like a good place for us to talk about The Game Called Life."

Lizzie crossed the street to a bench and just that moment was bathed in the warmth of the early morning sun. She laid on her back with her knees bent and sighed, "This was a good idea, Helen. Thanks."

"I *am* your helper, Lizzie," she responded.

"Oh, yeah. I almost forgot. A helper that inflicts bodily injury. It's a good thing I don't have too many helpers like you," Lizzie said smiling gently. "OK, let's talk about The Game Called Life."

Chapter Two

The Game Called Life

"You remember the games you used to play when you were a kid, Lizzie?"

"Yes...?" Lizzie said tentatively.

"There would be a board and little plastic or metal figures to represent various players and cards that you'd draw. They provided obstacles or rewards as you progressed around the board. Sometimes there was even play money. Sometimes you'd get a card that would allow you to progress quickly and other times you'd have a setback or even be sent to a pretend jail?"

"I remember," Lizzie responded, still wondering what this had to do with real life.

Reading her mind, Helen continued, "Well, what you call real life is much like those board games except it is what I think you call built to scale...it's a life-sized game. Nothing that you have been imagining is real and certainly not those things that you've been so concerned about like the house, the car, the vacations and the retirement. It's OK to have those things, as long as you understand they are just rewards along the way. The problem is that most humans begin thinking that they are the point of life. They aren't. In fact when people begin to think they are is usually when they totally forget that life is a game."

"Now imagine, Lizzie, how would your life might be different if you knew it was a game. Would you laugh more? Would you engage your sense of adventure more often? Maybe even linger on a sunset or the majesty of a heron swooping down across the lake behind your house? Would you be willing to put all your chips on the table for something that you really believed in?"

"That's a lot to think about, Helen."

"If you knew life was a game, would you laugh outloud when you discovered that the hurricane a few years ago was the answer to your prayers?"

"What!?" Lizzie asked incredulously. "I didn't ask for a hurricane!" she protested.

"Not in those words, Lizzie, but you did say you'd like to have a week to rest and relax and to get to know your new neighbors. When you didn't have electricity and businesses were all closed, you got just what you'd been wishing for...a whole week to recuperate and to get acquainted."

"You're telling me the hurricane happened just to answer my prayer?" Lizzie asked incredulously.

"Not just your prayer, but every single person got something they'd wished for in the month just before."

"Well, I could have done without a hurricane to get it. This is some game."

"People forget when they put out a prayer, it is their intention that is heard. Often the answer doesn't come in the form that they'd planned. A lot of people think their prayers aren't answered just because they

9

aren't answered in the way they had in mind," Helen went on." I think it would be best if I went all the way back to the beginning and explained the whole thing."

"That sounds like a dandy idea, Helen. Would you do that?" Lizzie responded.

"OK," said Helen, drawing a deep sigh, "Here goes."

"Lizzie you won't remember this because it is part of the set up for The Game Called Life, but it is important. Before you were born, you sat in Oneness with God and assessed the condition of your soul. Like watching a movie of the highlights of your soul's experiences, you noted patterns that you'd repeated again and again. They are what you might have heard called karma—habits that are attached to your soul."

Taking time to let what she was saying register to Lizzie, Helen went on, "Souls choose to come into human form in order to break away from those habits or work through the karma. Any time a soul masters a specific spiritual lesson, it carries the knowing with it through eternity. It never has to learn that exact spiritual lesson again. Souls are quite eager to eliminate as many lessons as possible because The Game Called Life gets easier with each mastery."

"You mean like past lives and all that?" Lizzie asked.

"Well, sort of, except that it is a game, and it is more like time-outs or half-time in a football or basketball game. You carry the score you have from one period into the next, but with time out to rest and reassess the lessons, the players—that's you souls in human form—get to start-out with a new perspective," the helper continued.

"Now in the spirit world, it is considered a great privilege to go back in the game to work on more spiritual lessons. Consequently, players must pay for the privilege. They pay with a promise to do special work that God anticipates will be needed. In order to do that special work, they will have had to learn at least some of the lessons that they set out for themselves. That adds extra incentive for players to complete their spiritual growth. Their soul benefits as it evolves, and all of humankind will advance as they complete their special life work."

"So you're talking about a calling or life purpose?" Lizzie asked.

"Something like that. Although it may, it doesn't necessarily have anything to do with work in the way you mortals talk about it. And it isn't really like a specific task. It involves a progression of assignments, each of which will help the soul evolve while giving back to the world."

"Is this like when I volunteered to work full-time for United Way that year? I worked hard all day but felt so good about what I was doing that some days I just felt I would burst with joy and pride about what we were doing," Lizzie added.

"Precisely! In fact, do you remember that time that you were moved to tears as you listened to the director of that child abuse prevention program?"

11

"I do!" Lizzie added excitedly. "She was telling the story of a little girl who had been severely abused when she was very young, but because of the program, the child was well-adapted by the time she got to school. What a heart-warming story!"

"Yes, it was. Your tears reminded you that it was time to look at your own history of childhood abuse, remember?"

"Oh, yeah. I'd almost forgotten. It was just after that presentation that I began to work with a counselor. Oh..." she said slowly, "I think I get it. My work for United Way was a contribution to the world, and in the process I got an opportunity to heal old wounds. Does that mean I got rid of some karma?"

"Absolutely! And the work that you continue to do to help others heal in this way is your payment for that. Learning your lesson prepared you to help others." Helen was obviously pleased that her reluctant student was catching on so quickly.

"So is that all there is to The Game Called Life?" Lizzie inquired, feeling herself growing more confident for the game.

"No, no. There is more, although it is a pretty simple game as it was created. People are the ones who have complicated it." Helen hesitated before continuing. "Now, as I was saying, a player's work is comprised of a progression of assignments, each requiring more spiritual mastery and more specialized skills than the one before. When the soul agrees to take on God's work, God in turn promises the soul to provide special gifts and talents that will be needed along the way. Souls must agree to develop those talents as fully and completely as possible because they will be needed for some or all of the assignments. If a player doesn't develop their gifts, their work must be reassigned."

"I'm not sure I understand," Lizzie pondered.

"Well, Lizzie, let's take you for example. What are your natural gifts?"

"Gosh, I don't know. I can't really think of any. Do some souls come without special gifts?" she asked.

"No, Lizzie. At least one (and usually more) special talent is standard equipment for being in The Game Called Life," Helen explained.

"Hmmm! What could my special gift be?"

"Lizzie, you have been richly gifted. Look around you at your home and your garden and the beautiful food you prepare," Helen reminded her student.

"You mean just stuff I do around the house could be a special gift?" Lizzie said with great skepticism.

"Your special gift is bringing beauty into every day life—making the ordinary sacred."

People often remarked about her beautiful home, but Lizzie had always thought they were just being polite.

"Lizzie, it is very important that you honor your talents. God is very proud of what you have done in this area," Helen said proudly. "But..." she stretched the word out as Lizzie cringed at what was about to follow, "you have been less responsible about some of your other gifts."

"I can't imagine others," Lizzie quickly defended.

"What did you like to do when you were young?" Helen asked.

"I played school. Even when I was in grade school, I really liked teaching the two little boys next door. When I got to high school, I started teaching the three-year-old neighbor girl Spanish as I was learning it. She learned almost as quickly as I did."

Lizzie was quiet for a moment. "Now that I think about it, I was almost always teaching someone something. I remember doing a cooking class on making chocolate chip cookies for the neighbor kids when I was in fourth grade. It's been a long time since I thought about that!" Lizzie exclaimed.

"You do have a natural gift for helping people grow. You have taken advantage of opportunities to encourage others on all of your jobs, but your next few assignments will require two other very important gifts with which you have done little, Lizzie."

"I really can't imagine what they'd be. Even the things that we've talked about don't seem special to me. They are things that I just do naturally."

"Lizzie, that's the point! Special gifts are things that you do well naturally because you have a talent for them."

"Well, we both know it isn't the piano. My mother tried to turn me into a pianist, but I always wanted to dance," Lizzie said, wistfully.

14

"Exactly, Lizzie!" Helen seemed most pleased.

"What?" she inquired, not realizing what she had said. "Exactly what?"

"Dance! Remember how you used to close the drapes when the family would be gone and play music and dance till the tears rolled down your cheeks?" Helen reminded her.

"I'd forgotten. I really did long to study dance, but I'm too old to start now and not very coordinated either. And besides what kind of assignment could God have for me that would require me to dance at my age?"

"Excuses, Lizzie. Excuses. In order to win in The Game Called Life, you must live with no excuses. And, you can *never* know what will be required of you. In The Game Called Life, only three things are important."

"First, you must learn the spiritual lessons that you agreed to work through. Second, you must fully and completely develop all your special gifts and talents. Third, you must do the work that God puts in front of you. That's it. Each player made a covenant with God to do those three things. There are *no* excuses for not doing them because nothing else is real."

"I don't get it, Helen. You're telling me that a decade after most professional dancers are washed up, that I should learn to dance because God has an assignment for me which will require dance?"

"I am telling you it is your responsibility to develop all special gifts and talents completely because they will be important to whatever assignment God has for you. In your case, that includes dance, and it would include dance even if you were 80!"

"OK. So I'll learn to dance. Any particular kind of dance that I'll need for my assignment?" Lizzie probed skeptically.

"Follow your heart. It is your compass to your own unique path," Helen encourage her.

"When I was younger, ballet really appealed to me. Now I think I'd want to do ballroom, but I don't have a partner," Lizzie explained.

"That's an excuse, Lizzie, and The Game Called Life is living without excuses."

"Hmm." Lizzie reflected to herself, "This is quite a challenge." Then something else Helen had said occurred to her. "You said, 'In your case, that *includes* dance.' Do you mean that I have other talents that I haven't developed that I will need?"

"Uh-hmm. That's right, Lizzie."

"I've never thought about myself as very gifted. Now all the sudden you are pointing out all these gifts I have to develop. When will I have time?"

"Players in the game of life often fill their time with other activities to avoid feeling the pain of ignoring their natural talents. When they follow their hearts, many of the other activities drop away."

"I can't imagine what could possibly drop away. Everything I do is necessary."

"What about all the time you spend cleaning your house which is already spotless? How about all the times that you've gone to the theater or a concert just because you'd be expected to be there when you would have really rather stayed at home and read a book?

"And, how about all the time you spend doing your make-up...sometimes three times a day...just so you'll always look perfect?"

"I think I get it, Helen. Maybe we could talk about my other gifts."

"Do you remember when you were a kid and liked to go with the adults to church instead of with the kids?" Helen inquired.

"You really know everything about me, don't you? I'd forgotten that."

"Lizzie, I told you I was your helper. I've been debriefed on your whole life and especially where you made choices that impacted your covenants with God to be in The Game Called Life."

Helen continued, "Do you remember what you did in adult church?"

"That's been a very long time, but let me think. I'd sing and do what the adults did." Lizzie said tentatively.

"Yes!?" Helen was so excited and sounded as if she expected more.

"Is there more?" asked Lizzie.

"Yes!"

"I can't remember anything special...Oh, I remember! I used to make notes on the back of the bulletin about what the preacher said! That's it, isn't it, Helen? I used to go home and write essays about the sermons. Is that it?"

"That's it, Lizzie! You have a gift for writing about complex spiritual issues."

"Writing about complex spiritual issues? Helen, if you've been thoroughly debriefed, you know I've hardly been in a church except for Christmas Eve and Easter for 20 years. I am not exactly what one would call an authority on theology."

"Excuses. Excuses! The Game," Helen started.

"I know, I know. The Game Called Life is living with no excuses. So at 40 with no background since childhood, you are telling me I am to become both a dancer and a theologian?" Lizzie was a bit exasperated.

"Life without excuses...and by the way, I did say writing about complex spiritual issues, not a theologian. There is a difference."

"There is? Don't I have to become a theologian to write about complex spiritual issues?" Lizzie inquired.

"My job is to help you identify your gifts and to get you back on your path. Your job is to listen to where your heart will guide you and live without excuses."

Lizzie had begun walking toward home, dawn now having fully turned into day.

"Lizzie," Helen spoke.

"Yes?"

"Lizzie, I will be here any time you want to talk, but if I recall correctly, you have an important meeting this morning. I wouldn't want you to be late, so I am about to disappear."

"Disappear? Helen, I never could see you."

"Well, in a manner of speaking. By the way, Lizzie, remember that in The Game Called Life every one you meet is there specifically to help you with one of your three agreements."

"Three agreements?"

"Yes. Completing spiritual lessons, developing your talents or gifts, and doing your special work."

"OK. So you are saying this potential client is not really a client at all but is here to help me do those things?"

"Exactly. He is masquerading, if you will, as a client in order to help you complete your work. And it is not just this one, but every single person in your life."

"You mean even the letter carrier and the paper boy?"

"Everyone."

Lizzie sensed that Helen was fading away, "Helen, how can I talk with you more? There's so much more I want to know."

"Just imagine being at one with me, and I'll be there."

"What does that mean?" There was no answer. "I guess I'll figure it out when I need to," Lizzie thought to herself. "What a start to the day." It was just then that Lizzie remembered her injuries. The pain had really diminished as she and Helen had talked. Her head spinning as she entered her front door, Lizzie winced as she turned the door knob with her scraped hand.

"What if life *were* just a game, like Helen had said, and my house *is* just a piece on a game board. Hmm. Everyone in my life is there to help me with something specific. Interesting thoughts." She wondered to herself. "Could it really be?"

Chapter Three

Redefining Success

Basking in the warmth of the spring sun, Lizzie savored each bite of her white chocolate macadamia nut yogurt. Her mind had been abuzz all morning as she reflected on the most unusual start of her day. One question kept echoing in her consciousness: What if life *were* just a game? As she reflected upon the possibilities, the prospects became increasingly extraordinary. There was so much she wanted to ask Helen, but she wasn't really sure how to contact her. Finding a quiet section of the park, Lizzie recalled Helen's words before she "disappeared" this morning.

"Just imagine being at one with me, and I'll be there," her helper had said.

Lizzie wasn't sure what that meant, but she imagined drawing Helen's voice into her. Before she had hardly completed the thought, Helen's familiar tone cheered her, "Great job, Lizzie. I was wondering when I'd hear from you again."

"That was easy," Lizzie remarked with surprise at how immediately Helen appeared.

"Players have a whole network of support just eagerly waiting to be asked, but they forget to ask. We are pledged to not interfere unless we are asked," Helen explained.

"What?"

21

"Oh, we'll talk about that later," Lizzie's helper knew there was so much they needed to talk about first.

Looking around her to make sure no one was in ear-shot, Lizzie began, "My mind has hardly stopped all morning. I have so many questions to ask that I hardly know where to start."

"How was your meeting this morning?" Helen interrupted.

"Well, that was just part of it. All the time I was talking to Sam, my potential client, I kept remembering what you said: every person that comes into my life and every event that occurs is to help me complete my covenants with God. It just seemed so strange."

Lizzie stopped to gather her thoughts. "Sam just seemed like any other potential client, but toward the end of our meeting, we started having a more casual conversation. Then he mentioned that he and his wife had just started taking a ballroom dance class. He said they did something called 'rotating partners' and that allowed those who came by themselves to learn the steps, too. I could hardly believe what he was saying. It seemed so bazaar that he might have called me to consult with his company just so that I could learn about their dance class. He seemed sincere in his conversation about his company."

"He was, Lizzie. Our learning partners don't know they are playing this role. Their lives feel as real to them as yours does to you. They just find an inexplicable urge to share a piece of information with you, like Sam did about the dance class.

"Many times, people will come in our lives for several reasons. If you end up doing work at Sam's company, you may find other things that you were to learn. If you don't, then you will know that learning about the dance class was the only reason for meeting him. Other times the work may be delayed months or even years until all the circumstances are right for what both of you have to learn from each other.

"In The Game Called Life a lot of things change, Lizzie. Perhaps the most important is how players define success. When we talked this morning, you defined success as a comfortable place to live, reliable transportation, a vacation or two a year, and food to eat. Now you are seeing that success at The Game Called Life is much bigger."

Helen continued, "A complex set of situations and people come together every day to help you learn the lessons you came here to learn, develop the gifts you were given, offer opportunities to prepare you for doing your work, and to assist others in experiencing those same things. Each one might be called a 'main event' of life. Success at The Game Called Life occurs when you show up for a 'main event.'"

"Now wait a minute, are you saying that Sam telling me about his dance class was a main event in his life? It doesn't seem like much to be labeled a main event," Lizzie remarked.

"In the fictional world in which you have been existing, it may seem like just an insignificant remark. What made it a main event was that Sam was assisting in doing God's work in you. By helping you develop your special gift, he was facilitating your service to the world. In some small way he was changing the world with a simple remark.

"It was also a main event for you because you heard it in this way. If and when you choose to go to the class, that will be a main event as well—and not just because you go to a dance class. It is a main event because you are demonstrating the courage to take the first of many steps toward your special assignment even though you don't know when or what it will be.

"Most likely that you were of service to Sam with one of his own lessons. In The Game Called Life there is no competition, everyone is always helping other players," Helen continued explaining.

"Think of it as scoring points. This morning both you and Sam scored points."

"I don't know what I could possibly have done to help Sam," Lizzie protested.

"And he doesn't know what he did to help you! Players have no way of knowing. It is possible that one of his spiritual lessons is to trust his intuition. He may have had a hunch to tell you about their dance class. When you responded with interest, it reinforced his trust in his intuition."

"I had no idea, but now that you mention it, he did seem quite pleased with my interest," Lizzie added.

"So are you saying we succeed at the game of life without even knowing it? It isn't much of a game if players don't even know what they do to win."

"You are right, it wouldn't be much of a game if players just stumbled along not knowing how to succeed. Yet, that is how most players participate in the game. Their karma has lulled them into an autopilot trance in which they have forgotten what is real, just as you had done before we started our conversations. Wake-up calls, like your fall and our conversation, are important because they give players an opportunity to remember what life is really about."

"You mean there are a lot of people walking around talking to invisible helpers?" Lizzie asked.

Helen laughed, "Not exactly. You specifically asked for help. Most wake-up calls are much different. There's a part of the contracting process with God that we haven't talked about yet that will serve your understanding of how players improve their chances for success. Then, we'll talk about the wake-up calls.

"At the moment a player completes a covenant with God to learn particular spiritual lessons, to develop special gifts, and to complete service work in the world, there is perfect Oneness with God. Those commitments are intentions—goals of the soul. That feeling is stored in the heart of each and every player that chooses The Game Called Life. Your intentions become what I described to you this morning as the compass of your heart. That feeling tells a player when they are at one with their soul's goals. The individual feels totally alive, energized, and invigorated. It is the feeling of Oneness with God or integrity.

"Conversely, Lizzie, when a player is out of integrity or not aligned with their soul's intentions, they feel bored, lifeless, and often fatigued, going through the motions of life. Often they feel like they are caught on a treadmill going faster and faster on a road to nowhere. They keep achieving the goals of their karmic drives, but they feel empty instead of energized by their accomplishments. Instincts tell players that they are off-target, but many are so consumed by living on autopilot that they are powerless to stop the cycle."

"Is that what happened in my car last week when I asked for help? I was out of sync with my soul's intentions?" Lizzie was intrigued.

"Precisely, Lizzie. The hopelessness you felt was the compass of your heart speaking to you. The fullness you experience when you create beauty in your garden or the way you present food is another way that your heart speaks to you. In those cases it is telling you that you are in integrity with your soul's intentions."

Helen took a moment before going on. "A player's emotions are their guide to success. The joy, peace, love and delight that you associate with an openness of heart is telling you that you're on the right track. Boredom, anger, frustration, and fear are warnings that you are off track.

"Emotions always carry important messages about what players need to change to be on track. No matter what is happening, Lizzie, a player is always capable of experiencing joy if they remember that every experience and every person is serving their intentions. Remembering that is a main event, and you might say scores points toward success in the game."

"You mean that when that schmuck left me with his secretary, I was supposed to be joyful?" inquired the eager student.

"Of course, Lizzie, for many reasons. It was a wake-up call, remember. However, look at all the things that have happened to you because he left you."

"I did go back to school which allowed me to get a better job in a bigger city where I have many more opportunities...including the chance to learn to dance!" Lizzie realized.

"Maybe you will even stop calling him 'a schmuck' now that you realize he was a helper in getting you back on your path," Helen chided.

"He's the last person that I would have ever thought of as a helper, but now that you remind me, life has been much more promising since he left. Even as I think about it, I feel more joyful. So is there more about how we win and lose The Game Called Life?"

"Many players get distracted from their real work here and begin to believe the monotony of their karmic existence is all there is. It is painful for them to see those who are in integrity being so fully alive. Consequently, instead of serving other players as they live their intentions, destructive players actually will try to impede those who are in integrity by discouraging them. Remember your college counselor who told you it wasn't realistic for you to become a writer? He told you writers were poor and starving, and he distracted you from developing your gift," Helen explained.

"What happens to those players?" Lizzie asked.

"Each case is different, but they build up more karma for their next round of the game. It is like losing points, and the score carries forward into the next round. The farther they get in the hole, the more work they must do to dig out. They lose points for distracting others, and they fail to gain points for either helping another or for doing their own work.

"Some destructive players have a wake-up call or other awakening, and then they work very hard at changing their lives. Others lose ground in The Game Called Life and will start the next round farther back than when they started this one."

"If my conversation with you is an unusual wake-up call, what is an ordinary one?" Lizzie queried.

"Wake-up calls come in many forms. Sometimes they occur as a serious illness or injury. Other times the death of a spouse, child, or a close friend will be the alarm clock. There is a wide variety of options but the purpose of the wake-up call is to confuse players enough about what is real that they will turn to God for answers. In those black moments, they often find integrity, and if they find the courage, they will follow the compass of their hearts." Helen seemed to stop, leaving Lizzie a few moments to reflect.

Taking a deep breath, Lizzie finally asked, "What happened when I missed all of those wake-up calls you told me about?"

"You just seemed to ignore the blackness. It was as if you were numb. You didn't want to hear. At the time you moved and decided to volunteer for United Way for three months, you also talked about wanting to write. That was a promising time, but you used your 'to-do list' to keep you so busy that you never allowed yourself to hear your heart," Helen sounded very sad.

Lizzie reflected, "Helen, that must have been disappointing to you."

"Shall we say I was challenged to keep you on course," her guide responded. "It is my job as transition helper to assist people in hearing their inner compass. Nothing I tried seemed to wake you," she said, hesitating briefly. "But you certainly seem eager to make up for lost time now."

"Helen, I am really sorry that I made you feel like a failure. I just didn't know." Lizzie felt like crying but the tears wouldn't come, but she did notice a fullness in her heart that was unusual.

"Helen, I am noticing a feeling in my heart that is...well...different. It sounds funny but it feels...bigger somehow."

"Oh, Lizzie, that's wonderful. You are beginning to feel your integrity...your Oneness with God! That is the point of The Game Called Life: to keep that compass open to guide you at all times. Your intention to be in integrity with your covenants allows you to feel it. Do you remember what you were thinking or feeling when you started to notice your heart opening?"

"Well, I was feeling badly that I had caused you to fail. In that moment I decided that I never wanted to cause you or any other players to fail again. I always want to be what you call in integrity with my covenants," Lizzie reflected.

"Memorize that feeling and use it to make every decision. Earlier you said it wouldn't be much of a game if players didn't know how to succeed. What tells them if they are on track is the feeling you have now. As long as you feel it, you are winning! It really is a very simple game. All you have to do is listen to your heart, and it will guide you unfailingly."

"You mean my whole life I haven't been able to feel my heart?"

"Sometimes you felt it, Lizzie, and ignored or dismissed it. Other times you were so busy that you didn't notice it," Helen explained.

"I can't imagine that I could have been feeling like this my whole life and just missed it. I guess the good news is that I found it by the time I was 40! There's a lot more I'd like to know about, especially how I could have been so numb, but I've got a lot to digest here. Can I call you like this again, Helen?"

"Imagine being at one with me, and I'll be there," her helper assured.

"So shall it be," Lizzie said, suddenly thinking that was strange language. "Do you think..." she started to ask herself. "Could it be this had come from her heart—that she was speaking from her heart?" She was almost giddy at the prospect, wondering what people—er, other players—must be thinking as she glided through downtown, making her way back to her office. "Maybe they are celebrating with me!" she exclaimed outloud, laughing with delight at the prospect.

Chapter Four

Rewriting Our Stories

Lizzie breezed through her afternoon in the office, paying particular attention to holding her heart open. When she remembered that she was helping someone win at The Game Called Life while building more points for herself, she was surprised at how fast the time went and how much lighter tasks that she normally dreaded became. Two times when she was perplexed about what to do with a situation, she just held her heart open and asked, "What will keep my covenants?" Each time an answer—a surprising answer—just popped into Lizzie's head.

Moving through her after-work routine of errands and stopping at her favorite deli for dinner, Lizzie felt energy surging through her body and a real bounce in her step. Could life really be this easy?

It certainly felt like playing a game...and Lizzie was sure she was winning.

When she pulled into her driveway, Lizzie could hardly wait to walk in her garden. Her spring perennials were in full bloom, and as always, she was captivated by the hum of bees, birds, and butterflies busily doing their work around her. "Do you suppose they're in the game, too?" she wondered. She suspected they were. The prospect that she was helping them while enjoying her garden was compelling.

Making her way to a bench in the corner of her garden, Lizzie sat quietly and felt her heart expanding even more as she looked at her flowers and then just imagined Helen being with her.

"Lizzie, you are radiant. You are certainly winning at The Game Called Life today." Helen assured her.

"Helen, this has been the most spectacular day. I didn't realize life could be like this. I want every day to be like this," Lizzie told her helper.

"Just bring your intentions into your heart and it will be, my dear," Helen was obviously pleased.

"Helen, there is so much I want to ask you about that I hardly know where to start. My head has just been spinning, but I guess the question that keeps arising most often is 'Why don't we all live this way all the time?' Where did we go wrong?"

"It isn't that players go wrong, Lizzie. They just never went right!"

"What?? What's the difference?"

"Let me explain using a situation from your life. When you were growing up bread was important to meals in your family, wasn't it?"

"Oh, yes," said Lizzie. "We had bread with every meal. My mother always put a huge stack of slices on the table even though there were just four of us. Most of the time, we finished them."

"And as you reached adulthood, did you continue to eat bread?" Helen asked.

"Of course. I loved good bread. I began to be more interested in the quality than just the quantity, though.

Finding the bakeries with the best bread was a quest. I'd stop and pick up a fresh loaf somewhere several times a week. My favorite restaurants were ones with the best bread. But what does this have to do with The Game Called Life?" Lizzie asked curiously.

"We'll get to that part in a bit. Just go along with me. What happened three years ago?" Helen inquired.

"You know everything! Of course, I discovered I was allergic to wheat, which is the primary ingredient in bread..and a lot of other things I love to eat." Lizzie answered, still bewildered about what this had to do with her question.

"You had to stop eating anything with flour in it, right?" Helen probed further.

"Yes..." Could there be something else Helen was seeking?

"What was it like in the beginning?"

"*Very* hard. I'd find myself actually buying bread out of habit and then realize I couldn't eat it. In restaurants, I'd even butter bread and almost get it to my mouth before I'd notice what I was doing. Other times I'd just crave it. I couldn't get it off my mind," Lizzie had forgotten how hard it had been to give up one of her favorite foods.

"What encouraged you to stay with it, Lizzie?"

"Quickly what I'd assumed were pollen allergy symptoms went away...just at the peak of pollen season. Within three or four days I had more energy than I'd had in years. I felt great. I couldn't imagine that I could have been feeling like that all along and just didn't know how simple it could be!" Lizzie said, suddenly realizing what she'd said.

"I guess it is a bit like today, now that you mention it. I didn't realize how easy it was to feel like this until today," she continued.

"You are catching on, Lizzie, but let me fill in some blanks," Helen said, the demonstrable pride at her student's quick understanding was apparent in her voice. "In order for players to learn their karmic lessons, they must, hmm.." She struggled for the right words. "They need to pretty much pick up where they left off in the last round, so they won't have any memory of anything else in this life.

"In order, to accomplish this, when they are entering into their covenants with God, they choose a family and circumstance which from birth will reinforce karmic behaviors, beliefs, attitudes, and even expectations that they will need to change. Just like eating bread with all meals was automatic for you, behaviors, beliefs, and attitudes can become so much a part of us that we don't think about them. By the time players have reached the age of five, they are so deeply inculcated with their karma that they don't even know any other possibility exists. Their karmic patterns are all that they know."

"Seems pretty diabolical to me," said Lizzie.

Helen chuckled. "Well, it would be, if the players hadn't asked for it. Remember, Lizzie, the whole point of The Game Called Life is to evolve an individual's soul. Doing spiritual work is...well, work.

The only way a player can do that is first be consumed by their karma.

"In your life, for example, you are learning about commitment, trust, and faith. Consequently, early in your life, you encountered several situations in which you were either abandoned or thought you were being abandoned. That set you up to doubt people. As you got older, your karma was attracted to people who weren't trustworthy, reinforcing your history. Take the man you married, what is it you call him, 'the schmuck?'

"People who have mastered the lessons of commitment are very careful in selecting a mate. They look at their potential partner's history for evidence that this is an individual worthy of trust. You didn't do that.

"The karmic story that you told yourself was that if you were "just swept off your feet," the relationship had to be right. You told yourself a story about how he'd be different with you even when in your heart you knew the truth. Later you said, 'Any moron should have been able to figure out that he was going to boogie on you.' Maybe that was true, but certainly someone who was wide awake and not in a karmic trance would have known."

"This is part of your karma, Lizzie. It is natural for you to avoid commitment now because you have been hurt so many times. But, it is only by doing what has *not* been natural and automatic that you and others learn and grow. You will grow when you are more studied and careful about making a commitment to a trustworthy individual. You will grow even more when you learn to stay the course with commitments you have made."

"Stay the course? It wasn't me who left," Lizzie was irritable about her failed marriage.

"It wasn't you who left the marriage," Helen agreed, "but let's be honest, Lizzie. You were never completely in that marriage. You were always worried about Romeo leaving you and at times you even wished for it, believing you could do better. You would flirt with other men to reassure yourself that you could still attract someone else if he did leave you.

Your thoughts about him leaving you sent up a prayer for it to happen, and at the same time your doubt kept you distant from him. Neither of you allowed the closeness to develop that occurs in a deeply committed relationship."

Helen paused and allowed her words to sink in. She knew this was hard for Lizzie. She knew it was difficult for players to accept accountability for creating their own circumstances. They always found it easier to blame someone else. Finally, Lizzie spoke, "You're right, Helen. I didn't recognize it, but I never was fully in that marriage. This spiritual lesson stuff is going to be harder than I expected."

"Lizzie, accountability is a tough spiritual lesson for everyone and most every player confronts it in some way." She paused, concerned about whether to go on. She knew this was a bitter pill for all the players she'd guided.

Finally, Helen continued, "You have failed in many other commitments, too, Lizzie." She hesitated once again knowing this too would be upsetting to Lizzie. "Look at all the incomplete projects that you have around the house and how many people you've promised to spend time with that you never did. As much as you loved them when you were younger, your commitments to writing and dance are incomplete."

"I don't think about those as commitments," Lizzie defended.

"But they are. A player who understands commitment is one who does what she says. She carefully considers before making promises and then keeps them, whether it is to the quilt that you've been embroidering for 20 years or getting together with Janet for lunch like you've been promising for months."

"When you fail to meet your obligations, you fail in your covenant to support others. Take Romeo, for instance. If you had learned your lesson about studied commitment, you would have turned him away. Your actions, in turn, would have forced him to experience the consequences of his behaviors. You didn't, so he never learned and has continued his pattern.

Similarly, your grandmother really wanted to teach you how to quilt it before she died. Because you didn't do your part, you didn't allow her to share lessons she was supposed to teach. Unlike this morning with Sam when he did his part in telling you about the dance class, and you did your part in responding to the opportunity to develop your talent, your failures resulted in incomplete work for your Grandma.

"It is the same with Janet. You are a role model to her for work she is to complete. She won't know how to move forward on her lessons until you keep your commitment to spend time with her. By the way, you have something to learn from her as well."

"I had no idea!" Lizzie lamented, and as she did, she felt her heart begin to be fuller as it had earlier today. Then she realized that it had happened as soon as she'd made a conscious decision to be careful in making commitments and then to be faithful in keeping them. She was feeling her integrity again.

Helen sensed what was happening but waited for Lizzie to speak, "It happened again, Helen. As soon as I was in integrity with my covenants my heart started to swell."

"Ah, my dear, your compass is very reliable in telling you when you are on the path to success in The Game Called Life. "

"Helen, you've told me about the lessons of commitment, trust and faith that I must learn. Is that all?"

Helen practically snorted as she coughed her answer, "Oh, no, Lizzie. There are many more!"

"Did you say *many* more?"

"I did. There are many spiritual lessons for every player to master. Most will complete some and not others. Those which are incomplete will be picked up in the next rounds of The Game," Helen explained.

"So how can I possibly know all the spiritual lessons that I have to learn. I like this feeling of success in my heart. I want to feel it as often as possible. Is there a secret to discovering what I am to learn?" Lizzie inquired.

"Actually, Lizzie, there is a secret. Each player goes through their game with a 'story' about how things are. Let's call this the 'karmic story' because until it is challenged, it is all that anyone knows to be true. Let's go back to our simple example. Until you learned you were allergic to wheat, you assumed bread and mealtime went together, right?"

"Right. It was one of the most important parts for me," Lizzie agreed, trying to figure out where Helen was going with this one.

"And what happened when you went into a bakery or the wait person brought a basket of bread to the table?" Helen asked.

"My mouth would literally start watering. I could almost taste it. In fact, I am experiencing it now, just talking about it," Lizzie said, laughing, "and it has been three years."

"Back then, what happened when your mouth started watering?"

"I'd go for it. A lot of times I broke off a chunk of bread from the loaf before I got out of the bakery or

I'd have the clerk cut off a piece for me to eat on the way home. In a restaurant, I'd almost dive for the baskct. It's cmbarrassing to talk about it now. It was like an addiction. I couldn't control myself," Lizzie admitted.

"Those responses were all happening *without thinking* about them. You didn't think to yourself, 'It is time for my mouth to water.' Your mouth just watered and you *re*acted by getting some bread to it. You even said after you had given it up that there were times you found yourself buttering bread *out of habit* without realizing it."

"I did. It was really odd. Almost like I was hypnotized or something. That's it. Earlier you said our karma kept us in an autopilot trance. That is what you meant, isn't it? Act or react without being aware of what we are doing?" Lizzie was excited and proud at this discovery.

"Right. Your karmic story is what you do out of habit *without thinking*—without even being aware," Helen confirmed. "So awareness is the first step in learning a spiritual lesson because until players recognize their karmic story, they can't change it. The moment an individual observes that they are acting habitually, they are in the position to begin to change it. While they are on autopilot, they simply react to whatever stimulus is put in front of them, be it a basket of bread or Romeo or whatever triggers any part of a player's karma.

"The next step is to remember your soul's goals—your intentions, and then rewrite your story to reflect what your soul wants to learn. It becomes your divine legacy story—the one you intended even before you were born.

"Let's continue with the bread. Another of your spiritual lessons, Lizzie, is to be responsible for creating your physical health. This, by the way, is a lesson you are nearly mastering. We are all quite proud of you. When you rewrote your story in line with that intention, you said to yourself, 'I like good bread, and I like feeling good even better.'" Helen continued.

"You're right! Those are exactly my words," Lizzie was surprised and pleased with the recognition that Helen had given her for this successful work. It had been very hard to give up bread. After swallowing those bitter pills about commitment, she was ready for some acknowledgement of success.

"Once a player rewrites their story, they are almost home. The last stage is finding the will or discipline to create their intended future. This is the integrity piece. At this point, the player knows what to do but must directly transcend their habit—or karma— in order to do it. They must *act* in accordance with their intentions to succeed in spite of deeply ingrained autopilot trances. This is why it took you several weeks after you made the commitment to change before you stopped picking bread up out of habit."

Pausing momentarily, Helen continued, "You, Lizzie, like every player have many stories that you have unconsciously told yourself to support your karma. One of the reasons it was so unpleasant for you to admit that you had accountability in your marriage is because that truth discredited the karmic story you had been telling yourself about how you had been a blameless victim. As we talked, you were confronted simultaneously with both the fiction that you had been living and the opportunity to rewrite your story."

She allowed Lizzie to reflect on what she had just shared before continuing, "The moment you decided that you would always be more considered both about making commitments and keeping them faithfully, you rewrote your story to coincide with your divine legacy to be a woman who could be counted on to tell the truth. That moment of integrity is what swelled your heart open again. Your next test in The Game Called Life will be to exercise the will to be reflective and judicious about making any commitment. In The Game Called Life, it doesn't matter whether a player promises to do something significant or makes an off-the-cuff, 'Oh, I'll do that.' Each is a commitment. Keeping it scores points. Breaking even the smallest commitment makes a pinprick in one's integrity."

Helen let Lizzie reflect for a moment.

"You live dozens of karmic stories every day. All support your habitual way of living. For instance, you tell yourself that for your business to be successful, you must work hard, yet earlier today you experienced what it was like to work easy, light, and playfully."

"It was great!" Lizzie agreed, adding, "That's sure a story I want to rewrite."

"You tell yourself that it is important to take the shortest route to work and home at the end of the day. That's a story that supports your karmic habit of rushing through life. If you asked what would support your covenants, you might find yourself driving home through the park where you could take a few minutes to truly enjoy the beautiful plantings there, and maybe even get ideas for your own garden."

Finally, Lizzie spoke, "There is so much that I've never thought about."

Laughing, Helen said, "That's what I meant when I said players don't go wrong. They just never go right. Players pass dozens of choice points each day where they have the opportunity to rewrite the story that supports their habits and 'go right.' However, Lizzie, the nature of karma is that unless a deliberate decision is made to 'go right,' by default players will 'go wrong.'"

"I understand how it worked with the bread, because I knew I needed to give it up. And, you told me about my lesson with commitment, and now I *really* get that one. How does it work with some spiritual lesson that I don't know about?"

"Lizzie, if you remember, you didn't always know that you couldn't eat wheat. It was just three years ago when you discovered that. You discovered it because of your commitment—one that you have been most faithful in keeping—to your health. Do you remember *how* you discovered?"

"Sure. I had heard about people curing themselves of allergy problems. Mine had been really bad for the last two years. I'd tried a number of alternatives but none worked. Before Lent I prayed about what I should give up that would reduce my allergy symptoms. I was afraid that the answer would be gardening or running or something I enjoyed outdoors. The answer to my prayers came very clearly, 'Don't eat wheat!' Within a week all of my allergy symptoms were gone!" Lizzie remembered both how astounded she had been and how great she suddenly felt.

"In any single moment, Lizzie, every player is always facing a choice point. Whatever is happening, there is always the option to continue autopiloting through their karmic story. At the same time, the player can intentionally choose to live their divine legacy story.

"Even when the player doesn't know what specific spiritual lesson may be at hand, all he or she must do is what you did when you were preparing for Lent: ask for help. By simply holding your heart open in integrity and offering a short prayer, the player can ask what thought, word or action in this moment will serve all their soul's intentions. One choice point at a time, the successful player at The Game Called Life can be guided to create their divine legacy, without even knowing what specific lessons or tasks are at hand.

That, my dear, is the secret to success in The Game Called Life."

"Helen, it sounds like a successful player is praying all the time. How am I supposed to get anything else done?" Lizzie laughed at her question.

"Oh dear, Lizzie, now that's quite a question. I think you may need another break before we start talking about living a prayer. For now the most important thing is to remember that in The Game Called Life the only thing that is real is doing your spiritual work. Most of those other things that you want to do are part of your karmic story about what you *should* do."

With that, Lizzie sensed that Helen had "disappeared" again. She hadn't realized it, but the sun had set while they were talking and, she was sitting on her bench in the dark now. As she gathered her gardening tools and began to walk up the path to the house, Lizzie noticed that she was quite tired. It had been quite a day, a day that had turned her world upside-down or maybe it was right-side up. She wasn't sure which it was, but despite feeling tired, Lizzie felt better than she had in years. "Hope," she said outloud, "That's what it is. Maybe for the first time, I really feel a deep sense of hope."

Her heart expanded again. She smiled as the gravel crunched under her feet, "I guess hope must be one of my soul's intentions. I can live with that. I even like the idea—life with hope. YES!!" she said aloud, giving a thumbs-up sign to herself in the darkness.

Chapter Five

Reconciliation

Lizzie found herself wide awake long before the alarm sounded the next morning. She noticed that her heart felt really big. She just lay there for several minutes feeling her integrity. Was it always like this in the morning, and she'd been missing it? She suspected it was or could be. For now, she just reveled in her fullness.

Suddenly Lizzie's mind flooded with commitments made over the years that she hadn't kept. Could it be that focusing on her heart had reminded her? As she was coming to understand The Game Called Life, Lizzie suspected it had. Smiling, she thought "Life is going to really be good now that I know what is real." Remembering the significant work she had to do, she added, "Not easy, but good...very good."

"I am choosing to be a woman who can be counted on to keep her word." Speaking the words Lizzie feel good to be stepping into her new story— what Helen had called her divine legacy. Reaching for the lined pad she kept in the nightstand, Lizzie began to make three lists:

- People I've made commitments to
- Projects I've made commitments to
- Things I've committed to doing for myself

Feverishly making notes under each column, Lizzie found it hard to keep up. Each time she added something to one of the lists, two more would come to her mind. She kept holding her heart open but wondered aloud, "How will I ever catch up with years of broken promises?"

Just as she did, Helen suddenly "appeared."

"Lizzie, it took you 40 years to get here. You can't expect to right all your broken obligations today!"

"Oh, Helen, I hadn't expected you," Lizzie said with a start.

"You held your heart open and asked a question. That invites divine support, so here I am."

"I guess I did ask how I'd ever catch up. The sheer magnitude of this list is astonishing. What a wake of failed commitments I've left behind me. I am really disappointed in myself."

"Lizzie, that is the past. It is critical to success in The Game Called Life to remain in the present. Who you have been when you were living your karmic story is no longer what is important. All that counts now is who you are choosing to be—a woman who can be trusted to keep her word—right now. Since you have rewritten your story, you only have one commitment to keep."

"Only one? What about this list? I don't want a bunch of pinpricks in my integrity. With all the broken promises on this list, if my pinpricks were connected they'd make a hole about the size of the one in the Titanic!" Lizzie said with chagrin.

"The one is a big one, but only one. It is a commitment you make to yourself and your integrity—your Oneness with God."

"What is it?

"It is the one you made yesterday: to only make commitments you will keep and to keep the commitments you make. I think you will find yourself making many fewer now that you are aware of the long-term consequences. However, the first of those might appropriately be to 'right' all your broken commitments from the past."

"What is the difference?" Lizzie asked.

"How many broken commitments do you have on your lists?" Helen asked.

"Maybe 50...that I've thought of so far," Lizzie said with a bit of embarrassment.

"What does it feel like to have 50 things to do?" Helen queried.

"Almost overwhelming. Like I can never finish...and I keep thinking of more."

"Lizzie, in your work, you often have big projects with many parts. How do you successfully complete them?"

"I start by breaking them up into smaller parts, prioritizing the sections by deciding what needs to be done first. Then I develop a plan and work on one thing at a time. One day, all that is left is a lot of loose ends, which are pretty easy to plod through, and suddenly, sometimes it feels like a miracle, I'm finished. I think I can see where you are going here, Helen."

"When you are working on your project, what do you start with?"

"The big, time-consuming pieces of the work that take a block of time. Some of the littler chunks I can fit in here and there when I have a few minutes before an appointment arrives or at the end of the day when I am too tired to start something demanding more concentration. Are you saying that I should start with the really big things? I thought that I'd knock off a lot of little ones real quickly."

"That's OK, Lizzie, but how do you feel when you complete one of the really big segments of your project?"

"It gives me a boost, energizing me for the next big section. I see your point," Lizzie admitted.

"You may find that you want to do some of both. Perhaps make a list of big promises that need attention and a second of items that will be quick to complete. Prioritize your list of big items, maybe even breaking them down into segments from which you can celebrate partial completion. Use the second list like you would in your office, when you have a few minutes here and there. You may even want to create 'a few minutes' in your day by getting up 15 minutes earlier. That will give you almost two hours each week to complete little projects."

"But we are getting a little ahead of ourselves here, Lizzie. The first thing that you want to do is assess your list. See what you can learn from the list about how you got into these commitments that you didn't keep. You can use these broken promises to add details to your divine legacy story."

"You mean there is more to the story than being a woman who keeps her promises?" Lizzie asked.

"Well, if you think about it like a book, Lizzie, that tells what the book is about—like the title. You have a lot to learn about what it will take to become a woman who keeps her promises. What you learn along the way is what adds depth and dimension to your new story—like each chapter of a book adds understanding about its subject. When you have finished the book, you know much more than you did from just reading the title."

Helen went on. "Take a look at your lists and see what you can learn very quickly. Then I'll show you how you can add it to your story."

"The first thing I notice is that I don't think about what is involved: how long it will take or what it will cost. I also notice that I've committed to a lot of things that I *can* do but don't necessarily *want* to do."

"That's great, Lizzie. Anything else you notice right away?" Helen probed a bit more.

"I'm not quite sure how to put it, but it's about consequences. I don't think about what I am going to have to give up that is more important to me when I make the commitment. For example, I told Kitty that

I'd help her put her bookkeeping system on her computer. I *can* do that, but I really hate to work on the computer...and especially bookkeeping...even for my own business. What is worse is that I've been promising myself—a commitment I've broken to me—that I wanted time to read all the books that I've bought and haven't opened. In the time I'd be helping Kitty, I could be reading. I just haven't thought about the consequences when I agree to do these things."

"Great, Lizzie. So what have you learned that you *do* want to be sure to do in the future *before* you make a commitment?"

"First of all, I want to make sure it is something *I* want to do."

"How will you handle it when someone asks you to do something you don't want to do?"

"Hmm. I suppose that I should first check with my heart to see what will support my covenants."

"Excellent, Lizzie, and then..." Helen was obviously pleased and excited.

"Unless I get clear guidance that it is something my soul intended, I guess I should keep my intention to be honest and just tell the person that my heart wouldn't be in it."

"Yes! Yes!" Helen's student was clearly a quick study. "And what if it is something you want to do?"

"I should ask lots of questions about what it will take, when it is needed, and then ask for time to think about it. I am sure if I'd really taken time to think about most of these, I wouldn't have made the commitments.   That will allow me the space to contemplate what might be a more important use of my time and energy. Now that I think about it, that's how I never got around to writing. It wasn't that there wasn't time. I simply allowed myself and my writing to be the lowest priority."

"Great, Lizzie! Any time a person rewrites their karmic story, it is necessary to look at the old story and learn from it and then *consciously choose* what behaviors you will select instead for your new story. Now there is something else that you need to do with that list."

"What's that?"

"You've already mentioned that there are things on your list that you didn't want to do. Mark them in some way. What do you notice about them?"

"Well, first of all I notice that there are a lot of things, like that quilt, that I wanted to do when I started, but really have no interest in any longer. Actually, I also notice some things that had deadlines or pertained to events that are long since history. Others are things that I agreed to because I like the person, like Kitty, but just didn't specifically want to do what I promised."

"That's a great start. Now it is time for you to learn another spiritual lesson. This is a big one for most players, as well."

"I'm not finished with commitment, and you're telling me about another one?" Lizzie said as a grimace gave way to a grin on her face.

"Lizzie, commitment is probably one you will be working on most of your life, and like I told you yesterday, each player has many lessons to work on simultaneously."

"OK, Helen, what is this one?"

"Lizzie, this is the lesson of forgiveness. Forgiveness is God's nature, and each soul is made of God's nature. Players forget their true nature when they are trapped in their karmic stories. Rewriting the story that players tell themselves about forgiveness permits their true nature to emerge.

"When players are trapped in their karma, they often see the world as a great competitive stage, but as we've seen in the real world we are all here to help each other. From their competitive perspective, they often tell themselves that it is a sign of weakness or failure to either give or ask for forgiveness. It is just the opposite. Players are reflecting their godliness when they forgive. They give others the opportunity to step into that role when they ask for it. At the same time, forgiveness liberates players from the burdens of guilt, blame and shame—qualities that make individuals forget their godliness."

"Let's start with looking over your list of things that are history. It is too late to keep those commitments. What you can do is use them as a platform from which to build more trusting relationships—another spiritual lesson you have before you. So pick one item from that list and let's look at it, Lizzie," Helen requested.

"I committed to sell tickets for the Rotary Club Duck Race last fall. I took the tickets, but I don't like to sell things so I never tried. The money goes for great causes, and the chair worked hard to make it a success. I really let him and the club down."

"How do you feel about that, Lizzie?"

"I'm embarrassed and ashamed...disappointed in myself."

"OK, Lizzie, now you get the opportunity to work on several spiritual lessons at the same time. What was the chair's name?" Helen asked.

"Gene," Lizzie responded with anguish.

"When you get to this item on your list of priorities, call Gene, and tell him the truth."

"You mean just tell him I took the tickets and didn't even try to sell them?" Lizzie asked.

"That's what you said the truth is, didn't you?"

"Yeah, but..." Lizzie sputtered.

"No buts, Lizzie. This is spiritual work, and you are learning the consequences of broken commitments. Tell Gene the whole truth, though. Not just that you didn't sell the tickets, but that you are disappointed in yourself, even embarrassed and ashamed. Tell him it wasn't honest of you to even take the tickets. Tell him you know he worked hard to make the project a success and the money goes for many worthy causes. Then, ask him to forgive you, keeping your words as simple and clear as possible, 'Will you forgive me?' If he forgives you, which he probably will, then simply say 'Thank you.'" Helen continued to explain.

"That seems simple enough," Lizzie said, "and just thinking about it makes me feel better."

"Finally," Helen said.

"You mean there is more?"

"Yes, Lizzie. There is more. Ask Gene what you can do to make it up to him *that doesn't involve selling anything*! And be certain that you don't commit to doing anything that you won't do."

"It seems like a lot with all of these items, but it feels really clear and clean. It will be important for me to remember that each item is just one piece of a big project so I won't become overwhelmed."

"Good, Lizzie. It may even be useful to keep your original list so that you can see how many items you have crossed off. But, Lizzie, there are other items on your list that will require different kinds of forgiveness."

"Oh, yeah, I almost forgot."

"Lizzie, let's take that item with Kitty and the computer bookkeeping project. Once again, you want to call Kitty and be honest. Tell her that you really like her and you want her new business to succeed, but in your enthusiasm, you offered to do something that you really don't like to do. Consequently, it hasn't happened. Simply ask for her forgiveness. Then offer to help her find someone who can assist her and be both knowledgeable and excited about the bookkeeping project. You probably already know someone." Helen advised.

"You're right. I know exactly the right resource for her."

"Once again, you want to offer to make up for the inappropriate commitment. If it feels right, offer to do something to support her in her new business that feels more in keeping with your covenants...like writing a press release for the local newspaper about her new business."

"That's a great idea. Then I get to support Kitty *and* my own commitment to writing. I love it. Maybe I could offer to do something like that for Gene and the Rotary Club, too."

"In these examples, Lizzie, you are learning several lessons. One of course has to do with coming clean on your commitments, but you are also learning about forgiveness, relationship- and trust-building, and keeping your intentions to yourself. In The Game Called Life, players often find that when they are keeping all their covenants that one action serves fulfilling several intentions, just as you've seen here."

"Is it a good idea for me to actually ask myself if there is a way I can use each decision and action to serve multiple intentions, Helen?" Lizzie wondered.

"It certainly is. That will almost always point you in the right direction. Now, dear, there are a couple more things about forgiveness, and then you'd better get ready for work!" reminding Lizzie that time had been passing quickly as they talked.

"There's more about forgiveness?" Lizzie inquired.

"We've just been talking about asking for forgiveness. There are two other kinds of forgiveness. *Eventually,*" Helen emphasized, "you will want to make three sets of lists for forgiveness, just as you've done with commitment. You don't need to do this right now. If you attempt too much at once, you may become overwhelmed. Your karma will want you to believe that you can't win at The Game Called Life and will try to convince you to give up and fall back into the autopilot trance where you don't have to think about what you are doing. As you've already discovered, being fully in The Game is both much more fun and much more rewarding, as well."

"Now, I'd better get on with this or I'll make you late, and I don't want to cause you to break any promises to clients," Helen continued. "You will want these three lists:

1) People you need to ask for forgiveness, like those we've been talking about with whom you have broken commitments or in other ways have hurt;

2) People you need to forgive, like Romeo and maybe people who have broken commitments to you or in others ways hurt or injured you; and finally,

3) Things for which you need to forgive yourself. That will include broken commitments to yourself, but also things that you may be carrying some guilt about. You may find some overlap between list 1 and list 3. Both steps are important, so include any appropriate items in both places.

"You mean that I have to forgive my ex-husband?" Lizzie demanded incredulously.

"You don't *have* to do anything, Lizzie. But think about the burden your resentment has been for you. Isn't it time you freed yourself from that? Besides didn't you tell me yesterday how much better your life had been since he'd left? Maybe you should thank him!" They both laughed.

"I see your point, Helen. My resentment has hurt me, not him."

"In each case, keep forgiveness simple. Just ask a simple, direct question, when requesting forgiveness, 'Will you forgive me?" For people you want to forgive, simply say, "I'd like to forgive you for...," if that feels appropriate. In some cases, you may be out of touch with the individuals or they may even be dead. Then simply sit with your heart open until you can see their face in your mind's eye, and either ask for or give forgiveness."

"Helen, there are some people that I think may take offense if I forgave them, because I don't believe they even know they did something that hurt me. Would it be OK for me to do that with them, too?"

"Of course, Lizzie. The whole point of forgiveness is to free *you* of guilt and blame so that you can freely connect with the individuals in the same way that God connects directly with you...Now, Lizzie, there are more things on your list that will serve us to forgive: those are the items that you are no longer interested in and failed commitments to yourself."

"I'd almost forgotten. There are quite a few of them," Lizzie reflected.

"Let's take that quilt, Lizzie. Tell me about it," Helen invited.

"I started it while I was in high school. I took it on during a time when I was discovering a variety of sewing handiwork techniques. When I bought the kit, the picture looked pretty, but I didn't realize that almost one-third of the pattern was embroideried French knots—something I didn't like to do."

"Ah," said Helen. "This is another place where it would have served you to ask more questions before you made a commitment. Would you have purchased the kit if you had realized it had all those French knots?"

"Most certainly not!" Lizzie said indignantly, then laughing at noticing how strongly she still disliked the idea of tying French knots.

"I completed most of the rest of the embroidery work, but every time I'd start to work on those knots, I'd get bored and put it away for a few months. Eventually, I just stopped taking it out. As I got into my twenties, I was much more active physically and enjoying the outdoors and nature. Sitting and sewing no longer interested me. I know Grandma really did want to teach me how to quilt on my own project. Every time I'd visit, she'd ask about it. We were really close. I feel quite badly that I disappointed her." Lizzie sighed.

"That is the past, and you can't change it, Lizzie. The Game Called Life is the present, and we can change it," Helen advised.

"What am I to do?" Lizzie inquired.

"Remember that 'What am I to do?' question to start with," Helen laughed. "By simply remembering your intentions and asking that question, most often you will know what to do. You can do it anywhere and any time. You won't need to ask me, because the answers are always in you. Let's try it, Lizzie."

"What do I do?"

"Simply state your intentions to complete the specific lessons you came into The Game to learn and ask, 'What am I to do about my broken commitment to my quilt project?'"

"OK." Lizzie repeated Helen's words, and suddenly said, "WOW!!"

Helen laughed and asked, "What happened, Lizzie?"

"The very instant I asked the question, almost before the words were out of my mouth, I knew exactly what to do! I am to forgive myself for incompletely researching the project before I bought it. Next I am to forgive myself for not completing it. Finally, since Grandma is dead, by holding my heart open I am to ask her forgiveness for not allowing her to teach me how to quilt my project. All of this feels just right, Helen, but the last part was a little odd."

"What is it, Lizzie?"

"This morning I am supposed to take the incomplete project to St. Mary's Episcopal Church and give it to them. I don't go to that church, and I don't really know any one who does. It seems an odd thing to do," Lizzie said, almost embarrassed at her "silly" words.

"Lizzie, when you ask what you are to do with an open heart, you will always receive the Highest Guidance. It is *very* important to follow it *exactly* as it is given to you," Helen advised.

"You mean *that* church even though I don't know anyone there and specifically *this* morning?" Lizzie continued to explore.

"*EXACTLY* as it is given to you," Helen strongly reinforced.

"OK. I'll do it, but it seems very odd," Lizzie relented.

"Promise?" Helen pressed.

"Promise!" Lizzie laughed. "This is really important to you, isn't it, Helen?"

"Lizzie, it is really important to *you!*" Helen emphasized to her recalcitrant student. "Now, Lizzie, we have another group of items on that list that we need to review. Those are the commitments that you've made to yourself that you *did* want to keep, but haven't. How about that reading stack?"

"I have a whole shelf of books that I've purchased which I've never had time, er, I guess it would be better to say, I've never made a priority to read. I already know that if I were more careful in making other commitments that I would have more time, and from what I know now, I suppose that I should assess the time I have before buying more books. But now, I have a lot of books that I want to read that I haven't gotten to. What am I to do? Oops, there is that question again!" They both laughed.

Lizzie continued, "I suppose now you are going to tell me I should ask myself."

Helen laughed again and said, "Lizzie, you are learning very quickly. Remember I am only here to aid in your transition to consciously playing The Game Called Life. I won't always be here to help you. It is important that you learn what to do when I am not here."

"OK, Helen, here I go." Opening her heart, Lizzie said the words, "It is my intention to learn all the spiritual lessons that my soul intended. What would you have me do about my reading stack?" Gasp! "It happened again. Before the words were hardly out of my mouth, I knew what to do."

Even though Lizzie couldn't see Helen, she sensed that she was smiling as her helper said most wisely, "And what would that be, Lizzie?"

"Again, the first thing I am to do is to forgive myself. Does this always happen? I mean, the forgiveness part?" Lizzie queried.

"I told you it was a *very* important lesson for most all players to learn."

"OK, so I forgive myself—first for buying more than I could read and then for letting other things that were unimportant keep me from even picking them up. Then the next part was most interesting."

"Tell me about it," Helen invited eagerly.

"Since I changed the way I eat three or four years ago, I almost always wake up long before the alarm goes off in the morning. I am rested, but I've told myself for so long that I needed eight hours sleep that I usually just lay in bed being lazy or maybe dozing a bit. Wait a minute! I just got it. That I need eight hours sleep is a karmic story, isn't it? It is a fiction that isn't true since I changed the way I eat. I get it now. These things are everywhere, aren't they?" Lizzie said, demonstrably excited.

"Yes, they are. How wise of you to notice. This transition period will be most successful if you begin to notice your karmic stories everywhere in your life. Being aware of the stories will allow you to break the trance and rewrite it according to your soul's intentions." Helen counseled.

"Now that I think of it, the rest of my answer was about how I will rewrite the story. Does that happen, too? I mean the part about being told how to rewrite it?" Lizzie pressed on with her enthusiastic inquiry.

"Often the 'title' of the new story will come in this way. Sometimes if it is a simple story you are rewriting, as I suspect this one is, you will find most of it within you quickly and easily with this simple question." Helen informed her. "If the story you are to change is a bigger one, like changing your relationships to commitment in your life, there will be many aspects that will require a great deal of reflection—asking questions and listening, but more of that later. I am most excited to learn how you will rewrite this story."

"In the future, I will get out of bed the moment I wake up. I will get ready as I always do, and when I've finished eating my fruit for breakfast, I will sit and read until it is time to go to the office. Most days that will give me over an hour to read. On Saturday morning, I usually linger even longer, sometimes two or three hours. If I do the same thing on Saturday, that will give me nine to ten hours each week for reading! I will probably be able to finish at least one, maybe two, books each week." She described her new story enthusiastically.

Then Lizzie slowed a bit, "But once again there was part I didn't understand. There are a number of those books that I bought years ago, and like the quilt, are no longer appealing. I am to sort through my books and remove the ones I no longer want to read. Then I am to call my friend Carol and offer to give them to her. I don't understand it."

"And, Lizzie, if this is your guidance, do you need to understand it?" Helen chided.

"No. Just follow the directions *exactly*," Lizzie laughed.

"That is a wonderful new story you are writing for yourself. In order for it to be most successful, it usually helps players to identify related karmic stories that may prevent them living their divine legacy story.

What will keep you from getting out of bed when you know that is what your soul intends for you, Lizzie?"

"Oh. I know exactly what it is. The story that I tell myself is 'I work hard and I deserve to lay in bed a bit longer.' I tell myself that one a lot on Saturday morning when I am being very lazy." Lizzie admitted.

"That is a story that will be important for you to rewrite in order for your new reading story to be successful. What is the new story you are going to tell yourself when you wake up?" Helen said, inviting her student to integrate the several lessons the helper had introduced.

"Hmm." Lizzie pondered, "I know. I will tell myself that I deserve to read all those books that I've been wanting to read and to know everything I'd know if I had."

"Very good, Lizzie. When you master all that we have talked about you will not only have rewritten your story to be a woman who keeps her promises, but you will also be a forgiving one who keeps relationships clear and clean."

"That's the way I want to live, Helen," Lizzie said, a bit contemplative.

"Lizzie, that's your soul's intention. That is what you came into the world to learn. Now that you know how to fully rewrite your story, you can start doing it at every choice point. Now I must disappear, or you'll be late, my dear," Helen chided herself.

"Helen?" Lizzie didn't want her to leave quite yet.

"Yes?"

"Helen, thank you. I love what I am learning, and I love The Game Called Life!"

"Lizzie, it is *my* privilege."

Chapter Six

Integration

Looking at the clock on her nightstand, the bright red letters told Lizzie that it was later than she normally started getting ready. She jumped out of bed where she had continued to sit while talking with Helen and straightened the covers, taking a moment to artistically arrange the pillows and teddy bear that she always placed on the bedspread. Lizzie found herself taking just a moment to truly appreciate the gift which Helen helped her identify: the ability to bring beauty to her home. It still seemed like such a little thing to her, but when she took a moment to really honor her uniqueness, Lizzie felt her heart swelling. Laughing to herself, she thought, "That's definitely a sign that I am on track!"

After Lizzie finished her routine of morning stretching, she closed her eyes and paused a moment as she said, "God, you know I haven't been very regular about talking to you for a long time." She hesitated before continuing, "Please forgive me." The words felt good to her as she remembered Helen saying, "It is God's nature to forgive." She really felt it.

"Thank you, God, for your forgiveness. I commit, and I intend to keep this promise, to bring you back into my life. Since I know now that the only things in my life which are real are my relationship with you and my spiritual lessons, I plan to live that way. Thank you for answering my prayer from last week and sending Helen." Then remembering what Helen had told her about the importance of inviting help, she added, "Will you help me stay on track?" Sitting quietly, for just a moment, she closed, "Thank you."

Lizzie felt an unusual mixture of peace and delight as she went through her morning ritual. Standing outside her front door before walking to her car, Lizzie once again asked, "Would you please keep me on track?"

Just as had happened with Helen, the words were hardly out of Lizzie's mouth when she had a flash, "I'm supposed to take that quilt to the church today...no this morning. Geez, I am not even sure I know where it is." Once again the words were hardly out of her mouth when she had a mental "snapshot" of a tattered old blue bag on the top shelf of the spare bedroom closet. Do you suppose...? She smiled, grabbing the step stool from the kitchen as she headed back to the bedroom. Sure enough, as soon as she opened the closet door, she spotted it just as it was in her "snapshot."

Driving to work, Lizzie found herself surprised to be remembering several additional broken commitments. Jotting them down on a scratch pad she kept in her car console, she wondered how long this would go on and whether she'd ever make them all up. Then recalling what she'd learned from Helen,

Kay Gilley

"They're all just pieces of one big commitment: to be a woman who makes commitments she plans to keep and keeps the promises she makes." Saying it felt good.

By the time she made her normal stop for a latté at the Hole-in-the-Wall deli across from her office, Lizzie remembered that she'd promised the proprietor several weeks ago to look over a press release he wanted to send to The Daily Record.

Before she could even order, Herb smiled, "You are seeming unusually chipper today, Lizzie. The usual?"

"I'm having a fabulous day, Herb, and no I think I'll do something different. Make it skinny today," Lizzie said, remembering her commitment to her health. "But, Herb, before you start that, I realize that I never got back to you about that press release you asked me to look over." Taking a deep breath, she added, "Will you forgive me?"

"Ah, sure, it's no big deal. I know you're really busy. I just stuck it back behind the register here." Pulling it from behind the old-fashioned hand-cranked machine, he added, "It'll be waiting for you when you have time."

Looking at her watch, Lizzie noted that she had almost 45 minutes before her appointment arrived, "Herb, I'd like to look at it right now." Taking the handwritten release from Herb, she sat at a small table and read through it. There were several small changes

70

that she noted. By the time that Herb brought her latté to her, she was finished.

Explaining the changes to Herb, she took a moment before continuing. Attentive to her new story about remembering to assess the time new commitments would require before making them, she added, "Herb, if you trust me to get it back before you retire, I'd like to take this and redo it on my computer," making fun of her delinquent editing job.

"That'd be real nice if you'd do that, Lizzie. I know a lot about making lattés and fruited chicken salads," he said hinting at his mastery at making her favorite just the way she liked," but I don't know much about computers."

"Herb, you always take really good care of me. It will be a privilege to do something for you." Halfway out the door, Lizzie recalled that she hadn't paid Herb.

Spinning in her tracks, she apologized, digging into her purse, "Herb, I'm sorry. I was thinking about the press release, and I almost forgot to pay you."

"It's on me today," he said, adding, "You go on having a fabulous day and let me be part of it."

"That's really sweet of you. Thank you, Herb, and I *will* have a fabulous day."

As she crossed the street and entered her building she realized that it had taken less than 10 minutes to keep that commitment. "I can't believe I didn't do that weeks ago," she thought. After turning on the lights in her office, Lizzie sat right down and entered the press release in her computer. It was coming out of her printer as the door opened, and her 8:30 appointment walked in.

* * * * * * *

"If you'll wait just a minute, I'll walk out with you," Lizzie said to her new client, "I have a couple errands to run. Slipping into her jacket, she picked up the faded and shabby blue bag and the press release and walked out the door as they continued to chat about Ted's project.

Smiling, she said, "Ted, it's been a delight. Life is too short not to have fun, so let's really enjoy this work together."

"This sounds like something I could certainly stand to learn," Ted laughed as they parted ways.

Thinking to herself about her words, Lizzie liked the idea about having fun on the project but couldn't really recall ever having said those words to a client. "Do you suppose this has something to do with one of my soul's intentions?" she whispered to herself as she crossed the street to the Hole-in-the-Wall Deli. "Well, I guess I can rewrite any story I want, and having fun in my work sounds like a good place to start."

The mid-morning coffee break crowd had packed the tiny restaurant, and there was a loud hum of conversation. Lizzie knew much of the downtown business community that frequented the place and spoke or waved to several people as she made her way back to Herb at the register.

"Herb, how's your health?" she asked.

Furrowing his brow as he tried to figure out the question, Herb paused before asking, "Now what are you up to, Lizzie?"

"Well, Herb," she reached into the small portfolio she was carrying. "I've got your press release done, and I wanted to make sure your heart was strong enough to stand the shock!" she joked with him.

"What!" the aging man feigned to be passing out as he held his heart, "I'm not sure I can handle this!" Herb and Lizzie both laughed. "Seriously, Lizzie, thank you so much. You've been so supportive of me ever since I opened this place. This is a BIG help. What can I get for you?"

"This is a great place, and you're a wonderful asset to those of us who get overly serious about our work down here. I'm glad I could help. I have somewhere else I need to go right now, so I'll have to pass on your generous offer."

"Thanks again, Lizzie," Herb shouted as she headed toward the door, "The next fruited chicken salad's on me!"

Realizing that her heart was swelling again, Lizzie took a moment to savor her newly-discovered compass. "Having fun with life is going to be OK. No, it's going to be better than OK. It's going to be great!" Not realizing she was speaking aloud as she almost bumped into the couple who managed her building.

"What's going to be great?" asked Don.

73

"Life!" Lizzie shouted, heading off up the street.

"Are you in love, Lizzie?" called his wife Laura.

Smiling, Lizzie called back, "Something like that...only better."

"You'll have to stop by later and talk about it," Laura retorted.

* * * * * * *

As she made her way up the busy street, Lizzie was keenly aware of the warmth of the sun, the spring flowers, and the lime green of the budding trees. "What a wonderful day!" she thought to herself. "I should get out during the day more often." Before she knew it, she had quickly covered the four blocks to St. Mary's. Never having been in this church, she surveyed it, wondering which door to try. She discovered the large doors in the front were locked. Walking around the corner, she spotted a smaller side door facing the side street. The heavy door opened with surprising ease.

Looking around for an office, she didn't quickly spot one, but heard voices coming down the hall. Tentatively following the sounds of activity, she made her way toward an open door from which she could now identify the voices of a number of women, older ones she suspected. As she stepped into the door way, a shocked silence fell on the room as a dozen or so aging matrons stared at her. Finally, one white-haired woman, dressed neatly in a tucked white blouse, pleated plaid skirt, and matching cardigan sweater stood up and walked toward her.

Suddenly, Lizzie realized they were sitting around a full quilting frame, just like she'd seen Grandma use, each with a needle and thread in hand. "Have you come to join us?" the woman who was now by her side asked with obvious excitement in her voice at the prospect of adding someone under 80 to their group.

Her question jarred Lizzie, who was still in something of shock at seeing the quilting frame. "Well, not exactly, er, well yes. I mean. I don't know."

"Are you OK?" the older woman asked.

By now, Lizzie had gathered her wits about her. "I have this quilt that I started years ago. I will probably never finish it, and I, uh," she struggled for the right word. "I, uh, was told you might be able to use it."

Inviting Lizzie to the frame which contained a beautiful gold and red pattern that she recalled from her childhood. "Oh, a Texas Lone Star," she remarked. "It's one of my favorites." The women were surprised and pleased that their younger guest was well acquainted with their art.

"You know quilting!" remarked one of them.

"Sort of. My grandmothers and great-grandmother were quilters. I grew up with it. That's how I came to start this embroidered quilt when I was younger. As I got older, I lost interest in it. I thought it was time to get it to someone who'd love working on it as much as

75

Grandma would have. It looks like my advice was accurate."

All sets of eyes expectantly moved to the crumpled and aging blue bag, but Lizzie was still in a bit of a shock that she'd "stumbled" into a quilting bee.

Finally, her "hostess" asked, "Well, dear, are you going to show it to us?"

"Oh, I'm sorry, of course," she said, reaching into the bag for the first time in probably a decade or more. Slowly, pulling it out, she surprised herself with the beauty of the almost complete square on top. As if gathering to see crown jewels, the aging group gathered around. One picked up the top square. The others gathered to examine it.

Finally, one said, "This is beautiful needlework. These French knots are exquisite. Did you do this?"

"Why yes I did!" Lizzie said with a shocked pride. She was especially satisfied that the woman had noted the work on the difficult knots.

"You have a talent, young lady," she continued.

Lizzie laughed, thinking only this group would think of 40 as young, and said, "I did it a long time ago. I haven't touched it for many years. I wouldn't even know how any more."

"We could show you," one eagerly volunteered.

"Thanks for the offer, but I am sorry to say that I've just lost interest. I'd like you to have it."

Having sorted through the stack of partially completed squares, one announced, "We'll have this done in a month after we finish the Lone Star, but that'll probably be two to three more weeks."

Reaching in her handbag, Lizzie pulled out a business card. "If it wouldn't be too much trouble, I'd really like to see it when it is finished. Would you call me?"

Once again it was her tidy hostess that spoke, "Of course. You sure you don't want to work on it?"

"I'm sure. By the way, what do you do with these when you've finished?"

"I assumed that whoever told you about us would have explained," the older woman spoke. "This is a fund-raiser for the abused children's school. We make the quilts and then sell them, or sometimes people hire us to quilt partially finished pieces, like this one. Last year we donated $1800 to the program. Do you know about the school?"

"I certainly do! I have done fund raising for the school and strongly support their work. How wonderful that it helps a program I believe so strongly in." As the words came out of her mouth, Lizzie recalled Helen explaining that decisions in integrity often times served several intentions. What a discovery that this group was raising money for the school.

"I must excuse myself and get back to the office. I am pleased that my project is now in such good hands."

As she turned and walked toward the door, she realized that her hostess had taken her arm. At the door, she looked at Lizzie with a mixture of disappointment and hopefulness as she said, "Please feel free to stop and visit us any time," she looked at Lizzie's card for her name, "Elizabeth."

Careful not to make a commitment that she couldn't keep, "Most people call me Lizzie, and I'll keep that in mind."

As she walked back to her office, Lizzie was pleased that she had another item to cross off of her broken commitments list. Making her way along the streets, Lizzie was curious now about what would happen when she called Carol about the books.

* * * * * * *

"Carol? This is Lizzie Magill."

"Lizzie. How are you?" her friend squealed with delight. "It has been *such* a long time. What's been happening?"

After briefly catching up, Lizzie began to explain the reason for her call. After having been led to a quilting bee which was raising money for the abused children's school, she was eager to discover what surprising connection Carol might hold for disposing of her unwanted books. "I have a stack of brand new books, which have been sitting around for several years and never been opened. This morning I decided to weed out ones in which I no longer have interest. Many are business books in areas that I no longer work," Lizzie said to her friend who taught business at a small college.

Before Lizzie could even ask her for ideas about disposing of the books, her friend exclaimed, "That's wonderful, Lizzie. One of our professors spoke at the only business college in Cameroon and discovered they had hardly any books. Our faculty started a project to send them books. These will be a great addition, since they are new books. When can I get them?"

Once again, Lizzie was astounded at what she was hearing. Since she hadn't yet gone through the books, she was taken aback by Carol's eagerness. "I will go through them Saturday afternoon. We haven't seen each other for awhile. Do you want to meet for brunch Sunday and I'll bring the books?"

"That'll be perfect," Carol agreed.

"This is astonishing," Lizzie thought to herself, already feeling her heart swell with integrity. "I make a major step towards a commitment to myself, I reconnect with an old friend, I help others complete their special work in the world, and my books will be read by people who are eager to read them. Helen certainly was right about serving multiple purposes with a single action when we are integrity with our intentions."

Glimpsing at the clock on her desk, Lizzie realized it was almost time for her lunch meeting. Grabbing her portfolio and jacket, off she headed out the door and down the hall. Lizzie realized how much she'd been enjoying her visits with Helen and was a bit disappointed that she'd have to put the next one off until after work.

* * * * * * *

"Herb, this is Lizzie. Can you make up one of those special edition fruited chicken salads for me to pick up a little before you close at 7 this evening? I'll swing by after my water aerobics class and take it home with me."

"Sure 'nuff. Now don't you get waterlogged, OK?"

"I'll do my best. See ya later."

Lizzie really enjoyed this class. Most of the same people had been in the class for the two years she'd been doing it. They shared both fun and encouragement. Today was special though. Lizzie had been proud when Helen applauded her success at being responsible for her health. She hadn't even realized it was a spiritual lesson. By the time she learned it, she was a success. She silently hoped that she would be as successful with the new lessons that she was just finding out about—commitment, forgiveness, connecting with others, being of service. She wondered what others she would discover. Walking the short block and a half to the athletic club, Lizzie allowed her heart to swell with integrity again. She was liking the feel and looking forward to another visit with Helen later.

Chapter Seven

Living a Prayer

Energized by her work-out and satisfied by her salad, Lizzie relished her triple chocolate frozen yogurt for dessert as she watched the sun go down. Drinking in the fullness of the day, she sat her dish down, took a deep breath, and imagined Helen talking with her. As quickly as she had the thought, she heard the now familiar voice.

"Helen, I've been so excited to tell you what has happened," she started. "To start with I've completed two of my commitments and made progress on a third, but the best part had to do with the answers that I got this morning to help me with that. Oh, I almost forgot there was something else first," Lizzie was excited and talking so quickly that Helen had to slow her down.

"One thing at a time, dear. Now, what happened first?"

"As I was leaving this morning, I stopped and prayed for guidance in sticking to my intentions. Instantly I thought about the quilt that I was supposed to take to the church this morning. I'd almost forgotten. Could it be that was the answer to my prayer?"

"Mmm...could be," Helen responded mysteriously.

Lizzie puzzled a moment over the answer before eagerly continuing, "Then I realized I didn't know where the quilt was. Since I had an 8:30 appointment, I had to find it quickly. Once again I had a flash—almost like a snapshot—of exactly where it was in the spare bedroom closet in an old blue bag. That's exactly where it was, just like I saw it in the 'picture.' Could that be the answer to my prayer?" she asked again.

Once again, Helen gave her the same, "Mmm...could be."

"What do you mean, 'Mmm...could be,'?" Lizzie asked.

"That's part of a much bigger topic, and I want to hear about the discoveries you made today before we move ahead," Helen explained.

"OK." Lizzie was still intrigued, but went on. "I went to the church as directed this morning, and there was a group of old women who were quilting! I couldn't believe my eyes. They do quilting to earn money for the abused children's school, a program that I really believe in. Can you believe it, Helen? It was just like you said, when I was in integrity...and doing *exactly* what I was told...I fulfilled several intentions at once. I got an item off my commitment list, I supported a program I liked, and I helped the ladies do their special work, too."

"Well, you have made progress today, haven't you, Lizzie?" Helen was most pleased.

"That's not all, Helen! That aroused my curiosity. I hurried back to the office and called the friend I was supposed to contact about getting rid of the books I no longer wanted. You'll never believe what she told me," suddenly Lizzie realized what she'd said. "Maybe *you* would believe me, but I wouldn't have a few days ago," she laughed.

"Try me."

"Carol's faculty is sending books to a college in a foreign country that doesn't have books! She was really excited to get them, and I'm getting to reconnect with an old friend when I deliver them to her at brunch Sunday. Isn't it incredible?" Lizzie asked.

"I'm glad you are making such good progress, Lizzie. And you are right, I *do* believe it all. I think it is time for you to start on your next lesson. Let's start with this word, 'incredible.' What does it mean to you?

"Hmm. 'Wonderful!' but more. So wonderful that it's not believable," Lizzie reflected.

"What makes all this be 'not believable'?" Helen probed.

"Hmm," she was obviously struggling to articulate what made this all so incredible. "I guess there are two things going on. First are the instant answers to my thoughts. Like when I was leaving this morning and asked to stay on track and suddenly remembered the quilt, or even earlier this morning when I first got the answers to my questions about the quilt and the books. Not only were the answers instant, but precisely appropriate!"

"The second part is how connected everything seems to be when I'm in integrity...being able to meet several intentions with a single action. It is almost as if there were a great master plan, and as soon as I stumble into it, everything works out perfectly."

"Now, my dear," Helen asked, "what makes all that unbelievable?"

"It just can't be, or I think it can't be, or I used to think it couldn't be. I'm so confused right now that I really don't know what is true any more. Can you help?" Lizzie asked in frustration.

"Confusion is good!" Helen said proudly.

"It is?" Lizzie asked. "I've always thought it was bad. Maybe that's another story I need to rewrite."

"Distinct possibility, Lizzie. As long as players think they know how things are, they are usually in their fictional worlds, living their karmic stories. When players get confused, often they give up their old stories and turn to God to find Truth. Would you be willing to try what we did this morning and just ask?"

"Sure, but I'm not sure what I am asking."

"If you did know, what would you know, Lizzie?"

"Let me give this a try." Feeling her heart fill fully again, Lizzie started, "God, you know my intentions. What is the Truth?'"

Sitting in the stillness, Lizzie again heard an immediate answer, "What is unbelievable is what you have thought was real. It is the fiction. All that is real is your relationship with God, your spiritual lessons, and being of service. That is your divine legacy, and it *is* connected with everyone's divine legacy. In Oneness everything supports everything else."

"That's incredible!" Lizzie found herself saying automatically and immediately correcting herself. "I mean that is awesome. Could it really be?"

"Uh-huh, Lizzie. That's how it is. That is what the The Game Called Life is about, remember? It is easy and effortless as long as you stay awake against the force of your karmic trance. We mentioned this a bit yesterday, and you've been experiencing some of it today. The secret to staying awake is to *live* a prayer." Helen reminded her.

"I recollect that now. You said we weren't quite ready. I guess we are now. Each time you emphasize the word '*live*,' I am accustomed to 'saying' a prayer. What is the difference?"

"What *is* the difference, Lizzie?" the helper threw the question back to her.

"This again. Hmm. Does it have more to do with feeling it?"

"That's part of it. When you hold your heart open in fullness—or in integrity—you are One with all that is in the Universe. But there is more," Helen invited Lizzie to ponder more.

"You have said every thought is a prayer. I suppose living a prayer might mean staying alert to that. A person, er, player would be served by being conscious about what they are thinking, so they can choose what their prayers really are. Hmm. That's interesting. I didn't know that I knew that," Lizzie said, quite pleased with her own discovery.

"Lizzie, you know everything. When your heart is open, you have access to the wisdom of the Universe. All you have to do is ask, and the answers are there for you," Helen explained.

"Everything? Helen, I can't believe that. There are things that I know nothing about, foreign languages and...piano," Lizzie challenged, laughing at her futile attempts to play during her youth.

"Everything. You may not have the vocabulary to understand everything yet, but you have access to it," Helen clarified.

"I think you have most of the basics, Lizzie, but let me pull them together a bit. Maybe that will help you understand. There are really seven parts to living a prayer. Followed faithfully, they will unfailingly keep players on the path their souls outlined before this round of The Game Called Life.

"First is **integrity**, the Oneness with all that is when you open your heart and focus your intention toward it. Some people call it God. Others use the word Universe or Love. Some think of it as their deep inner knowing. The name that you put on it really isn't important. Know that it is always in you, you are always in it, *and* the Oneness is all that is real. Biblically, God is identified as "I am." When players remember the "I am," they know they are one with God. Connecting with their integrity—what you call the fullness in your heart—reminds players who they are and what is real. As you recall your experiences today, know that they are what is real."

Helen hesitated to allow Lizzie to absorb her explanation. "I am beginning to understand, and I have a lot of stories to rewrite before I master it." Lizzie confessed.

"Of course! You've been living in the fictional world for 40 years and the real one for less than two days. This morning I told you how important it was to stay in the present. This is why. If you begin thinking about anything you knew to be true in the past, you will automatically fall back into a karmic story. You can only be in Oneness in the present.

"In the beginning you may only be able to do it for short periods, but as you sustain your commitment— one reason understanding commitment is critical—the percentage of each day spent in Oneness will steadily increase. It is intended to be a lifetime pursuit, so you aren't expected to get it 24-7 right away!"

"I'm relieved. This almost seems like an attitude toward life, and as I bring it to everything, I will probably find it easier to complete my spiritual lessons and my special work assignments," Lizzie surmised.

"Most certainly! Are you prepared to move along?" Helen asked, wanting to make sure Lizzie was ready.

"I think so," Lizzie responded.

"You've already experienced much of this, Lizzie. We are just organizing it to be easier for you to remember when I am not around," Helen explained.

"You mean you aren't always going to be available to me, Helen?" Lizzie asked anxiously.

"No, Lizzie. I will be gone soon. My job is almost over. I assist in transitions, and soon I will have shared all you require for this one."

"Oh, no," Lizzie moaned, "I'm not sure I can do this without you."

"Lizzie, where is it essential to be?"

"Where is it essential to be?" Lizzie echoed. "Oh, in the present. I guess I did drift ahead a bit."

Helen emphasized, "I *am* still here. You have access to the wisdom of the Universe. All you have to do is **ask**. That is the second key to living a prayer...asking. When you ask, you invite the participation of the whole Universe. That means me, God, whatever helpers are assigned to you at any moment, and even human helpers who may have been waiting for your paths to coincide.

"Players often experience those situations as coincidences until they come to understand that everything is part of a bigger plan. If you hadn't been growing in awareness, you might have thought it was simply coincidence that there was a quilting group at the church or that Carol's faculty was collecting books. Now you understand these as coinciding events.

"It is essential to solicit answers which are specifically aligned with *your* intentions when you 'ask' for guidance. Otherwise you may get an answer, but since you are accessing all the wisdom of the Universe, it may be for someone else's intentions! After clarifying your intentions, ask a simple question for what to do next, as you have done several times with me and a couple times today without me. Keep your requests very simple. For instance, you might say, 'My intention is to keep all my commitments. What would you have me do right now?' You can do this any time of any day and any where, even silently in a meeting. All players must do is hold themselves in Oneness and ask a question."

"OK. I hold myself in integrity, state my intention, and then ask a question. I've been doing that, so I think I can do that part of living a prayer," Lizzie said with growing confidence. "What's next?"

"You've already done this part, too, Lizzie. It is to **listen intently.** Often people get specific word answers similar to those you have received to direct questions. However, other times the player may not understand the immediate answer, so instead of words, the answer will come as a 'sign.' Most players find it useful at crossroads to specifically ask for a sign about what direction will serve their intentions."

Lizzie interrupted, "What exactly do you mean by a 'sign'?

"Signs may occur as people who unexpectedly show up, new opportunities that present themselves, or even a sign on a billboard or a word on a license plate. A song that plays on the radio just after you've pondered a question or lyrics that continue to replay in your mind may offer direction. A conversation in which someone gives you appropriate but unsolicited advice may point the way. Some players even notice themselves giving others advice that they need to follow. There may even be a time when several people in a short period of time mention the same book to read or movie to see, which will have a message answering the question."

"I think I understand," Lizzie said.

"Usually the answers will come so quickly that some people may miss them, so you must be very attentive. Occasionally, though, there may even be a delay of several minutes or even days before the answer comes because conditions may need to be set right. That is what happened when I needed to complete my work with Bill before answering your prayer from last week. Players must listen *intently* or they may miss either the answer or connecting it will the question if the answer comes some time later."

"So far, so good, Helen." Lizzie realized how much about living a prayer she had already learned.

"We're already up to number four, Lizzie! Once a player gets an answer, then they must act upon the guidance they've received. There are two action steps. Number four is to **explore eagerly.** Living a prayer requires a sense of adventure, Lizzie.

"Players tell themselves that they must know all the steps which will be required before they can act. Often there are hundreds of steps, lessons to be learned and other players to be coordinated. It would be impossible to explain the complexities even if helpers knew exactly how things will progress, but usually we don't. We never know when players who may be needed might get stuck in a karmic story and not be available to play their parts. When that happens, those of us who make arrangements must scurry to find someone else with the right qualifications to substitute.

"A player will always be given the next step. From a limited karmic perspective, it may not be logical but will always lead to another step which will lead to yet another step. Eventually, players live their intentions—their spiritual lessons and special work—without ever being aware of how they were unfolding. Usually, they can look back and see patterns which weren't apparent at the time the events were transpiring. A player may even appear to lose ground only to discover later the opposite was true."

"Appear to lose ground? What do you mean?" Lizzie queried.

"It really depends on the circumstance. A player's business may sudden fall off, giving the appearance that progress is not being made. In fact, we may be freeing time and space for the business to grow to the next level. Another individual may be wanting a permanent relationship, and suddenly their mate breaks up with them, giving the appearance that they are going to be alone. In fact, the player may have learned what was needed from that relationship to move on to one with their soulmate. The break-up was necessary to 'make space' for the soulmate to enter. Exploring eagerly requires a willingness to take such changes with a spirit of adventure...and faith," Helen explained

"Oh, I understand now. I didn't know what was happening at the time, but about three years ago, my business really slowed down. I refocused on projects I enjoyed more and suddenly it exploded bigger than ever. Now that I think about it, after I reorganized my business I was probably more in integrity," Lizzie was realizing now how she had already been doing parts of living a prayer without even knowing it.

"You're right, Lizzie. That's why it took off so strongly after the adjustment. Are you ready to continue?"

"Sure!"

"The nature of the unfolding explains the reason for the second action step: **follow fearlessly.** Players will often be asked to take steps that don't make sense, may be totally illogical, and may even fly in the face of everything they have ever been taught or believed. That is because the goals of their souls will almost always require them to do something different than they would have done in their karmic story. If they are to *live* a prayer, they must follow without knowing why—something most difficult to do, especially for very intelligent players who are used to figuring things out."

"I guess this is a bit like going to the church this morning. It just didn't make sense for me to take a quilt to that particular church I'd never been to on a morning in the middle of the week," Lizzie reflect.

"You are grasping this well, Lizzie, and...today's actions were baby steps. When you live a prayer, you will be asked to do things that are less logical and more risky," Helen advised.

"Like what?" Lizzie asked.

"I cannot know, but if you are in integrity with your soul's intentions, you will be required to transcend the limitations of your 'karmic' logic. My advice is to follow your guidance *exactly*, and what transpires will serve your soul's goals."

"This sounds a little scary," Lizzie contemplated.

"There will be moments when you will feel sheer terror, and if you allow yourself, you can experience the unabated joy of Oneness at those times as well. When players start projecting dire consequences or anticipating needs that may never materialize is when they become frightened. Living a prayer works on faith. In fact, while players generally think of 'faith' as a noun, 'faithing' might really more appropriately be a present tense verb. It describes the action when players are following fearlessly."

Helen let Lizzie digest this new thought before continuing, "Are you ready for the sixth part of living a prayer?"

"The heat seems to get cranked up on each one. After 'follow fearlessly', I'm not sure I'm ready for more!" Lizzie laughed nervously.

"The next one does fly in the face of most karmic stories, and consequently, is a giant step for most players. If players live a prayer, they will inevitably face increasingly challenging lessons and at the same time progressively more important service in the world. When they are caught in their karmic stories, most players think very small about what they can accomplish for the world. Number six is to **risk greatness**." Helen waited a moment before going on.

"I am not speaking of greatness in fictional world terms where people reach a high level in their worldly work or make a lot of money. Greatness in the real world means speeding the evolution of humankind. Most individuals will feel like they stumble into greatness and describe it as "just doing what I felt passionate about." That is true. Players' passions are part of the compass of the heart. When followed, a sequence of assignments intensifies the service delivered to the world.

"Players are always prepared with a sequence of less demanding assignments. As they develop their special gifts, learn additional lessons, and follow fearlessly, their personal path of greatness summons."

"I don't understand why there would be any risk to greatness. It seems like greatness is something people would want," Lizzie reflected.

"Greatness itself isn't the risk. The risk lies in the willingness to consistently answer a call that usually cannot be understood. The path to greatness requires players to do things that may never have done before or at least do them in unconventional ways. Imaginative methods will inevitably expose players to the scrutiny of friends, family members, and even society at large and may tempt them to retreat to the safety of their karmic patterns. Players have an almost uncontrollable desire for the approval of those around them, and many who come very close to greatness give up the quest to please or appease those around them," Helen explained.

"I kind of understand," Lizzie said, but Helen sensed that she didn't really.

"Your former U.S. President Jimmy Carter is a good example of someone who has followed his heart fearlessly. What his heart told him actually made him a very lackluster President, but that was never where God intended his greatness to lie. The very behaviors that made him an ineffective president actually laid the foundation for his real work through the Carter Center, promoting democracy through elections all over the world and in eradicating many disabling and deadly diseases. The risk came from his willingness to heed God's call rather than doing what his advisers, the latest public opinion poll, or media critics may have dictated." Helen described.

"It's hard to think about the presidency as a stepping stone, but in his case I guess it was. That being a mediocre leader would be an even more important boost to his special work is even more illogical," Lizzie mused.

"And that is often the case, reinforcing the need to follow fearlessly. We're almost through, Lizzie. Are you ready for last one?" Helen asked.

"What could possibly follow 'greatness'?" Lizzie asked incredulously.

Helen laughed, "This one doesn't 'turn the heat up,' Lizzie, if that will make you any more comfortable. This one may actually turn the heat down for all the others. The seventh characteristic of living a prayer is to **savor the gift.**"

"You mean there's a gift for all this?" Lizzie laughed.

"Lizzie, there are *lots* of gifts. In The Game Called Life, the most important ones come when The Game is over and your soul has the opportunity to assess its growth. I cannot describe the joy experienced by souls who have been successful in evolving significantly when they review how far they came. But savoring the gift is not about the end of this round.

"Players receive many gifts each day while they're in The Game. When we first chatted, Lizzie, I told you that every single thing that happens, every circumstance that presents itself, and every person that enters your life does so for a reason. Everything is a gift.

"The stories that players have told themselves that bad things happen or that negative consequences occur is terribly disabling. Players become paralyzed by the prospect of unpleasant outcomes. Results may be unexpected, but they are never 'bad.' There is always a positive reason for everything. When players savor the gift, they acknowledge the contribution from whatever is occurring and *express gratitude* through their on-going prayer even before they recognize how it will serve them. When players find themselves in a traffic jam or a long line at the grocery store, and say 'thank you,' they are savoring the gift.'"

"What possible good could come from a traffic jam or a line at the grocery store?" Lizzie asked with a bit of a surprise.

"It is impossible to say, but there will always be a gift. Maybe the player just needed to slow down and take a deep breath that day. While stopped in traffic, they may notice beautiful flowers along the highway that would be missed zooming along at 70 miles an hour. The delay may actually prevent the player from being in an accident at another point in their journey. While in the grocery store line the player may meet an individual important to a lesson which is before them, or they may pass along a needed word or idea to someone else. Most of the time the player will never know, but it is still beneficial to acknowledge the gift."

"I think I get it. I remember being in the store a couple weeks ago when there were very long lines. I struck up a conversation with a very nice older woman. She later told me that she was 83 years. She seemed lonely and pleased to have someone with whom to talk. I guess maybe that conversation was important to her, and it made the time in line go quickly," Lizzie surmised.

"Exactly. The time passed quickly for you and she had the opportunity to talk with a younger person."

Helen continued, "When circumstances seem exceptionally challenging, demonstrating gratitude is even more essential because doing so acknowledges the onset of a period of deeper spiritual work. Eventually, you will see the gift if you look for it.

Faith is easier when players acknowledge the giving nature of the Universe whatever challenge is occurring.

"It's a good target to let two-thirds of your communication with the Oneness be thankfulness. Those of us who work for our players up here, often for years without thanks and even more often being disparaged for our most special gifts, respond well to gratitude. It makes us want to be even more collaborative. It's also good reinforcement for 'an attitude of gratitude' to express appreciation to other players for the many ways in which they support you."

Helen gave Lizzie a few minutes to reflect on living a prayer before she continued, and Lizzie seemed comfortable taking the space she needed. "Do you understand that players live a prayer in every moment of every day?"

"I conceptualize it. How do I do it?" Lizzie responded.

"Conceptualizing is fine for now. The terms 'spiritual discipline' or 'spiritual practice' imply the need for repetition by a student to achieve mastery. Just as you would when perfecting a new sport or a musical instrument, if you have the discipline to practice living a prayer frequently, mastery is assured. Staying awake is the key. Start noticing when you have fallen into an autopilot trance, and in that moment, stop and ask for guidance. Day after day, the time you spend in conscious communion with Oneness will incrementally increase. Do you recall that you said many pinpricks from broken commitments had created a large hole in your integrity?"

"I certainly do," Lizzie winced to just think about it.

"The reverse occurs when you live a prayer. Each time you consciously choose to live a prayer, you add back a tidbit of integrity. Over time, the fragments will restore your integrity to wholeness."

The time had come for Helen to tell her eager player that she was about to leave. This was always a sad time for her students. Their karmic trances prescribed the belief that Oneness was closer when there was a human-like voice to consult. No matter how much she told them it was always there, players inevitably had doubts. Successful ones soon discovered that she was right.

"Lizzie," Helen waited for a response.

"Yes?"

"Lizzie, I will leave very soon."

"I don't want you to go...and...I know you must. I think I am ready," Lizzie said tentatively.

"Before I leave there's something more I want to share," Helen started. "Lizzie, do you know what players are most afraid of?"

"Gosh, I don't know. Oops! I'm not supposed to say that, am I? I guess the thing they are most afraid of is probably dying," Lizzie surmised.

"That's a good guess. It is what most people think, but dying is *not* really what they are most afraid of.

What players are most afraid of is *living*," Helen emphasized 'living.'

"Afraid of living?" Lizzie was curious.

"Yes, Lizzie. Really living: pushing life to the edge of simultaneous sheer terror and unabated joy. They are afraid of breaking the karmic patterns and consciously choosing the life their soul intended because there are no rules to follow, no models to emulate. They are afraid to blossom from the buds of their trances to be fully awake, aware and alive."

"I don't really understand. Oh, I guess, I understand the part about no role models to follow, but I'm still not sure I get why people are afraid."

Helen continued, "Players' fictional or karmic stories keep them small, Lizzie. When players are small, they pretend they are not accountable for what they know they can do. If the world isn't the way they would like it, they blame others and feign helplessness.

"God doesn't think small, and your soul didn't think small when it chose your path for this life. The work that you and each player committed to accomplish before you came is essential to building a better world. You knew it then, and when you are awake, you know it now. You can no longer pretend to be helpless or make excuses. You can no longer pretend that someone else is responsible.

"Players like the illusion of control. Changing the world can only occur when they give up that illusion and turn to living a prayer. Being responsible while being out of control is unnerving for players who have assumed being responsible meant being in control. They are afraid to allow themselves to be led mysteriously through a labyrinth of stcps, not knowing where they will be led. That is how players are truly alive, and that is why they are afraid to be alive.

"The potential to change the world is in every one of you, *and* it *requires* every one of you. The impossible will happen magically as you allow yourself to follow the compass of your heart with the faith that *God* knows where you need to be, when you need to be there, and when you are ready to do what is required.

"Lizzie, your soul knows the Truth of who you are and why you came here. If you live in moment-by-moment communion that life will be yours. You alone have the power to rewrite your story. You alone have the power to be as big as you are. You alone have the power to win at The Game Called Lizzie's Life. Winning The Game is a choice point in each and every moment of every day: choosing the life you came here to live. Like all players, Lizzie, you are given free will, so the choice is yours. How *will* you choose?"

In that instant, Lizzie felt Helen's presence disappear again. This time she knew it was for good. She pondered Helen's parting words, "A choice I make in every moment. How *will* I choose?" As she reflected, Lizzie knew there was no longer a choice for her. "How could I hold the power to change the world in each moment and not exercise it? Of course, I will!" In that moment, Lizzie's heart expanded again, reminding her of who she was. "Yes!" she said aloud, "I *will* win The Game Called Life...and I *will* change the world!"

About the Author

Kay Gilley...the world's leading thinker on intention

Kay Gilley is a spiritual mentor to executives, entrepreneurs and professionals, where she plays the role of "Helen" with her clients. In her writing, public speaking and individual work, she helps individuals break out of habitual near-life experiences to rediscover life, foster latent creativity and reclaim their whole potential.

Kay has been described as the "world's leading thinker on intention." She says that means intention is the assignment God has given her to master at this point on her journey. To date, her homework has included writing four books on fear, courage, and intention. She describes writing The Game Called Life as the ultimate exercise in surrender...written in five days with passion that changed her life and her health. Kay is also a keynote speaker...and whatever else God assigns her as she embraces her own game called life.

Kay's first two books, *Leading from the Heart* and *The Alchemy of Fear,* guide leaders at every level to work and live more consciously. *Leading from the Heart* was named as one of five "Books to Work By" and *The Alchemy of Fear* has been recognized as one of the "Best Books of 1997." It is available in four language editions. *Choice Points—Seven Keys to Living with Intention* (forthcoming) and *The Game called Life* inspire individuals to step up to their divine legacies. Kay is also collaborating author of *The New Bottom Line—Bringing Heart and Soul to Business* and *The Courage to Care*.

You're invited to visit Kay at her website: http://www.intentional-leadership.com or contact her at her Durham NC office:

Intentional Leadership Systems®
5 Chelan Court
Durham NC 27713
(919)572-2879